Dying
to be Faithful

Dying to be Faithful

J. P. Mackenzie

iUniverse, Inc.

New York   Bloomington

Dying to be Faithful

This is a work of fiction. All of the characters, names, incidents, organizations, and dialogue in this novel are either the products of the author's imagination or are used fictitiously.

iUniverse books may be ordered through booksellers or by contacting:

iUniverse
1663 Liberty Drive
Bloomington, IN 47403
www.iuniverse.com
1-800-Authors (1-800-288-4677)

ISBN: 978-1-4401-1835-7 (sc)
ISBN: 978-1-4401-1836-4 (ebk)

Printed in the United States of America

iUniverse rev. date: 01/26/2009

To my dearest Lara and Lewis, in whom I delight.
I hope you enjoy your story.

Contents

A special thank you to Joanne Burgess for the use of her photo on the front cover.

1

Death on the Beach

The unrelenting fierceness of the sun, accompanied by the roaming of the flies on and around Sebastian's head, caused him to stir. At first, he lay still. The sound of the waves and the faintest touch of a breeze were all that he could distinguish over the noise of the flies. Then fear, as if being in a nightmare and realizing it is real, gripped him with a thousand hands. His eyes shot open. A pain in his head like being struck by lightening caused him to grimace and close his eyes tightly, as when smoke from a fire fills them. He sighed greatly and turning his head, he clasped it with both hands. The pain in his head faded, but further horror from this action caused his hand to tremble. As he released his right hand from his head, he noticed the hair was warm, sticky and matted. He brought his hand into view and it emerged before him shaking, stained with blood and mingled with sand. With his hand directly in front of the sun, the blood looked almost black. He placed his hand once more on the back of his head, closed his eyes, and again, lay still.

A recollection of Sebastian's last conscious moments slowly found their way back to him. Forcing himself to sit up with some considerable effort, he saw his sword trodden into the sand by his side. As the weathered blood-stained hand that held his head now reached for the sword, he remnants of strength in gripping this old friend and the veins on his arm became more prominent. Sebastian dragged the sword close to his body and sought its aid in trying to stand. As he stood propped up against his sword, the heat and loss of blood made him feel faint and he looked more like a man that was about to fall down than a man who had just struggled to his feet. He managed to breathe some full deep breaths but in lifting his eyes over the landscape his breath momentarily stopped; the monastery was destroyed. Wisps of smoke faintly danced into the air as the blackened stones stood desolate against the vibrant blue sky.

The Men of the North had come. Sebastian stood there motionless apart from his mouth, which moved as if he was speaking but no words could be heard. He would have cried if he had any energy. The comparison of the beauty of the monastery as it once stood and the present heap of ash and rubble left Sebastian standing on that small island in bewilderment.

Was it really gone? He thought.

The old grey stone building, its arched doorways and stone windows, the secluded courtyard now open and bare, forced to share its privacy with all of nature. Its cool porches were now exposed to direct sunlight, darkened corners flooded with illumination, the blackened masonry resembling a demonic sculpture of a paradise lost. Only the left wing and its stone columns stood almost intact, for there was little wood used in its construction and its walls were thick. Sebastian realized that the ordinary everyday activities of the last two years, once taken for granted, were all now memories of which none would ever be re-lived. This saddened him to the very core of his being, and he stood there still, the sea air blowing his dark brown hair across his eyes. Those eyes, once full of contentment and peace were now fixed, piercing and filling with anger.

Before he could think of questioning why all this should happen he remembered the artifacts that had adorned the chapel. Gold: that was probably the reason to the question 'why?'

Or more likely, he thought, *man's insatiable desire for gold; greed, and greed enough to destroy even that which is good.*

The very thought of this last sentence sent a chilling sensation straight through his whole body.

'The others,' he cried, 'where are the others?'

All this time (in reality it was only a few moments) his thoughts had been occupied with the monastery.

'How could I forget the others?' he kept saying to himself.

He was about to turn around when he involuntarily paused. A whole range of images flooded his mind's eye like a rush of blood to the head, his eyes opened wide – the images were grim.

Were they all dead? He thought. *Am I alone?*

In steadying himself, he found the courage that good men have to do what is needed in the face of horror or loss. He gripped the handle of his sword tightly. His knuckles were as white as his face. He closed his eyes.

'Give me strength O God,' he prayed as he turned away from the ruin of the monastery to the western beach behind him. It looked as though he stood there praying but it was fear that prevented him from action.

He opened his eyes. He fell to his knees. He stared. With both hands on the helm of his sword he bowed his head, just as the first tear began to fall he cried out such a groan of anguish the whole island was aware of his sorrow. The gulls screeched and flew out to sea. The breeze which blew the pale green grass on the windswept dunes gave the appearance of a myriad of arms outstretched to heaven, swaying violently at the injustice of the scene of carnage before the wounded Sebastian.

The brothers had been slain. The dark contorted bodies strewn across the idyllic beach made the horror of their murder even more unseemly. The beautiful fine white sand ran down from the grass-covered dunes into the turquoise water, which deepened to a midnight blue.

The beach now entertained the bodies of dead men. Murder was a foreigner to this island, until now. Now the blood of innocent men seeped deeper into the sand, a union nature was helpless to prevent.

Sebastian found it hard to breath, yet he found it harder to move, and mainly because he knew he had to.

What if there are others like me, he said to himself, *wounded but not yet dead?*

He moved among the dead seeking life. There were thirteen monks at the monastery on the Island of Ness and it looked to Sebastian that the other twelve had given up their gift of life, or more aptly, those of whom it did not belong had taken it from them. All hope of finding someone else alive was fading fast.

Brother Rastko laid face down half across a rock and half across the sand, his sword still in his hand. Rastko was easily recognizable due to his size. He was thick set and of an impressive stature and his sword was broad. Sebastian loved Rastko like a brother, not just in name but also in nature. They often enjoyed the other's company in work, in prayer, in rising early and walking across the island and along the beach. He was a friend in the truest sense of the word and Sebastian marveled at his approach to life, for whatever he found himself doing, he put all of his effort to that task. Rastko prayed longer and more earnestly than any of the other monks; he also fought harder. Although the monks were pacifiers by vocation, they were neither pacifist in belief, nor practice.

Sebastian struggled to turn Rastko over but he beheld his brother's broken body, for something heavy had fallen hard upon his left shoulder near to the neck and an arrow had caught him under the ribs. Sebastian fell on him in despair thinking Rastko was dead but the pressure on his chest caused Rastko to cough. Blood and saliva caught Sebastian's face as he looked down in amazement. Rastko's blue eyes rolled as he tried to focus on Sebastian's face, his blond hair shining so bright in the sun. Rastko lifted his right arm and placed his hand on Sebastian's face. Sebastian closed his eyes and felt the tender embrace of his dear friend; the touch was so weak. More coughing and spluttering caused Rastko's arm to drop to his stomach. Sebastian looked into his eyes and all mercy on earth cried out for help. Sebastian slowly shook his head but Rastko nodded faintly and tried to hold a smile through the coughing; his teeth and mouth speckled with blood. So much was said without a word being spoken as one friend knelt before the other. Rastko's breath was so deep he wheezed each time he exhaled. Sebastian looked up to heaven.

Take this cup from me, he thought in despair, but Rastko reached for Sebastian's hand, his eyes were full of desperation and Sebastian saw how much he suffered. Sebastian's left hand reached for his sword and placing it over Rastko's heart, he rested both hands upon it. Rastko closed his mouth but smiled. He signed the cross over his own body and closed his eyes. Sebastian looked out to sea. He drew a sharp intake of breath and in breathing out he drove that sword into the body of his friend and cleaved his heart. Sebastian wept in silence. He hung his head, both hands still clasping the sword, and there on his knees over the body of his dead friend he vowed to God never to lift up his sword against another. Sebastian had faced many bandits on his travels and enemies in war but he had killed for the last time.

Never again, he thought, *will blood be spilt by my hands.*

Sebastian was devout, meant his vow and would strive to uphold it but as soon as he had spoken those words to God, he wondered in his heart if he would honestly keep his vow to the end of his days. Rastko coughed no more. Sebastian in one day had lost a dear friend, the Bothers of Ness, and the monastery he had called home. He found himself praying, although not intentionally, the kind of prayer that forces its way out in a groan or a sigh.

'What am I to do?'

It was a prayer of deep need and Sebastian expected an answer. Again, he looked out to sea, his eyes half shut because of the brightness of the sun reflecting off the surprisingly calm waves. He tried to think but the pain in his head was becoming more severe, and after all that had happened, more noticeable. Sebastian turned and looked back along the beach sloping towards the grassy dunes to the remains of the monastery, which was slightly raised nearer the middle of the island.

I'm so thirsty, he thought, *and I need something to bandage my head.* Then without deliberately stopping to consider a plan, one task after another filled his attention.

I'll have to leave and tell King Orran of what has happened ... but first I should bury the dead. I should also check if any artifacts or icons from the monastery remain. Did they destroy the boats?

He was just about to stagger towards the monastery when automatically he reached for his sword. The vow that he had just made came suddenly to mind. He stood there with an outstretched arm and open hand a short distance away from his sword. Sebastian thought for a moment that his vow had perhaps been rash. Before he had time to regret the decision, he lowered his head once more to Rastko's lifeless corpse and reassured himself that the actions he took were correct. Although this all happened without Sebastian really thinking any of it through, one thought merely succeeding another, as when a man breathes without thinking he must. As Sebastian's hand closed and his arm withdrew just a touch, he found a reasonable argument for taking his sword firmly in his hand once more.

'Just to walk with ... and protection against wild beasts,' he said relieved.

This eased his conscience but not nearly enough as he would have liked, for he knew he was making his vow harder, if not impossible to keep with these frail arguments and that singular action of gripping his sword. There was in his own mind partial justification, for there were wolves in the land in those days, plus bears. With his sword at his side, he made his way back to the monastery, desperate for some water to both quench his thirst and clean his wound.

What once stood as the lively kitchen in the corner of the monastery now contained only some of its provisions. A barrel smashed on one side managed to hold half its contents, and pieces of bread and the odd bit of fish could be found amongst the ash. There was enough to provide Sebastian with the strength to bury the dead and this duty he performed with profound solemnity and with much love.

Before the night fell upon him, he gathered a few sparse provisions for the journey on which he had never expected to embark. Sebastian planned to leave Ness at first light and report to King Orran all that had happened; that the Men of the North were attacking the coast by boat. The King lived in a castle on an outcrop of land, which became an island at high tide. Given the rugged lay of the coastline, Sebastian believed he could reach the castle of Tanath much quicker by foot, down through the ancient wooded pathways and raise the alarm.

For now, however, he sat with his back against a crumbling wall. He was covered with his own habit and an extra layer from a half burnt mantle wrapped around his body. Apart from the looming clouds out at sea, the open night sky provided an unwanted chill to the air. It also enabled the moon to touch the landscape with a soft white glaze. Sebastian stared at the moon; it in turn caused a subtle light to reflect in his dark eyes hidden under his hood. His young face would forever bear in its lines the events of that fateful day. The stars shone like a host of embers disturbed from a silver fire blown far into the distant sky. Sebastian remembered Rastko and wept bitterly. He watched the moon disappear into the sea until the silver spine it cast across the ocean ebbed away into the darkness of the night. Sebastian closed his eyes, and from sheer exhaustion, slept in the silence.

2

Eramia

Before the dew had vanished in the morning sun and while most of the castle still slept, Eramia sat on the top stair under the back porch overlooking the garden. She sat leaning against a central pillar of the porch enjoying the solitude, listening to the birds sing and watching the insects move in and out of the flowers. On either side of her garden towering walls provided some protection from the salt air. There was only a small stone wall at the end of the garden because it dropped off quite dramatically into the sea forming a near perfect natural defence. From where Eramia sat, in the cool of the morning, she could gaze right out to sea. The ocean breeze caused the cherry blossom trees along both walls to gently sway, but it was overall quite sheltered. Eramia came to the garden, sometimes to think, sometimes to pray, but often simply because she loved the view and the aromas of each changing season.

The beauty of the garden matched Eramia's countenance. She was tall, like her father, but her physical features she inherited from her mother who died when she was young. Eramia's hair was a rich chestnut brown and adorned her head in ample abundance. It was straighter than it was curly, which was possibly due to its weight for she wore it down to her waist. Her eyes were dark and captivating. She had a beauty that was striking and it caused many men to marvel but only the bravest of them to dare ask for her company, for her beauty could also seem quite austere and unapproachable. Added to the fact that she was the King's daughter, Eramia, through both beauty and status, often felt quite alone.

The garden was Eramia's delight. Her dreams in the garden often involved her future love life, even down to the last detail. As the morning sun grew ever stronger, the rich fabric of her long velvet dress revealed its splendor. The purple was almost black in the shadows but of a bright hue in the direct light. Against the light grey stonework of the castle and the greens of the garden, Eramia looked quite the queen, even though she was still young in years and in Orran's opinion lacked the strength it would take to rule (although on this point Eramia disagreed with her father profusely). Many of Eramia's attributes suggested she could make a fine queen, for she always sought and loved justice, and the riches that were hers by right she held onto very lightly, learning from the garden that happiness is often found in greater measure in things which cannot be owned. Most of the people esteemed her highly, partly out of reverent fear and partly due to the kindness of her heart. If one day she would become queen, she would certainly rule to serve her subjects.

Eramia stood up and took a slow walk away from the shelter of the porch in amidst the trees, cherry blossom falling softly at her feet. Orran peered out of a window in the library and saw his daughter enjoying the sea breeze.

O, how she looks like her mother, he said to himself, pausing for a moment and smiling. The sudden call of another female voice abruptly interrupted Orran's thoughts.

'Eramia, Eramia,' a voice shouted, and from under the roof of the porch appeared a young lady with a long blond plait, wearing a flowing green dress tied around the waist with a belt of brown leather. The woman held up her dress with both hands as she ran to meet Eramia at the bottom of the garden where she sat on the stone fence.

'Now you decide to wait on me?' Eramia said laughing and smiling.

'Why did you not wake me, my Lady?' said Hannah, her eyes wide open and her face red from running down the garden. When Hannah had caught her breath, she managed a smile. Although she was Eramia's servant, they were also very dear friends. They only really talked this formerly between each other when they joked together or at some rare official engagement.

'What shall we do today?' Hannah asked.

'I thought about taking the horses out into the woods on the mainland, but my father said we weren't to leave the castle. There have been more reports recently that the coastal attacks are getting closer,' Eramia said.

'Do you think they will ever really come here and attack Tanath?'

'The castle hasn't seen war in over half a century. Besides, reports can be wrong, and I hope they are,' Eramia replied.

'Well, why don't we get the bows out and practice?' Your father greatly approves that you can use your bow well and if we are attacked we can defend the castle too!' Hannah said enthusiastically, firing her invisible arrows into the sky.

'You just want to beat me again,' said Eramia, raising an eyebrow and smirking.

Hannah smiled as if to say, *yes.*

'I shall meet your challenge and we shall see who has the sharper eye and steadier hand this day,' Eramia declared proudly with her nose in the air and her hands on her hips.

'I will get the bows. I think they are still in my room from last time,' Hannah said, walking back to the porch and up the stairs.

'If not, check the armoury,' Eramia called as Hannah disappeared through the low wooden door. 'And bring back some milk and food with you.'

Orran was still watching Eramia from the window; she was his only child and was precious to him. He stood with both arms outstretched and leaning against the walls on either side of the window. His body was a little back from the glass to remain in the shadows, the sun faintly highlighting the edge of his silver beard. He had a lot on his mind. As Orran looked upon Eramia once more, the thought of war caused him to sigh. He lent forward and felt the warmth of the sun on his drawn face,

Still, it may not come to that, he said to himself, wishing it to be true.

Reports of attacks along the coast had increased consecutively in the last four months and Orran knew he had to take action, especially as it was the season for kings to go to war. The people in his kingdom were mainly farmers and fishermen, but those who could fight did so with almost reckless abandon, their own safety not even a consideration. The people of Greenhaven had a reputation of determination and apparent fearlessness in battle, and this had maintained a relative peace for fifty or so years. The nations round about them called them *The Craels*, meaning in the old tongue of the islands, *The Knights*, or, *Men of War*, taken from the legends and stories of the islanders who first settled there centuries before. There were just fewer than two thousand men active in the King's own guard, but only one hundred and fifty dwelt in and around the castle.

'Straight from the oven,' Hannah said walking back into the garden, the bows on her back and a wooden tray in her hands, 'fresh bread.'

The two women sat on the stairs eating and drinking. Eramia called to one of the guards and asked if he could set up one of the targets at the end of the garden. She always asked for things politely, which made it difficult for people to refuse, and everyone knew it was really a command. Eramia's pale skin and large brown eyes almost ensured her help for anything from the young men in the guards. Not that she exploited others by her beauty for she often went out riding or walking trying to conceal her identity. She equated favouritism with injustice.

Eramia and Hannah, enjoying each other's company, good food, the garden, and a new spring morning, talked and laughed together. They loved to tell each other stories, sometimes new ones but especially the old ones, like 'Dalan and the Wolf,' 'The Red Ship,' or 'The Chronicles of Melton.' Both young women were very inquisitive. Many of their conversations consisted largely of questions, all needing answers in time. Their favourite topics of discussion revolved around adventures, their ancestor's history and when most serious, theology. Not the deep subjects which took up the monk's time, but again, questions.

'If God can do this, why can't he do that?' Alternatively, 'Would God do this, if such and such happened?'

Eramia had found herself out of her depth on numerous occasions when talking with Ninian, her father's spiritual advisor and chief abbot. He had a habit of not answering her questions directly, but instead he would raise new questions for her to ponder, which often led Eramia to find the answers to her original questions.

This always amazed Eramia and when she was a young girl Eramia thought Ninian was the wisest man in the world. Ninian continuously found time for Eramia and this also impressed her. His old weathered skin and balding head with unkempt grey hair failed to dim the life that she could see in his kind eyes. They were eyes that had seen much and told stories of their own. Ninian was old in years, and he spoke very slowly, pronouncing every syllable, but always choosing his words very carefully. Nothing trivial passed his lips and for this, all men trusted him. He had taught the King from Orran being a child and Eramia did not know life in the castle without him.

Fed and watered, Hannah turned to Eramia,

'You can keep talking if you like, but you're only putting off losing,' she said, grinning from ear to ear.

'Please,' Eramia said, with her arm pointing towards the target and the palm of her hand out, 'after you.'

Hannah stood up with her bow in her hand and three arrows by her side that she placed into the ground. She was fairly petite and slim with modest physical strength. Although she could not fire her arrows to any great length, her accuracy at shorter range was consistently impressive. Eramia and Hannah both knew she was the better shot, and it pleased Eramia to see her happy in these friendly contests. It did amuse Eramia, however, (not that she ever mentioned it), when she saw Hannah taking careful aim – the bow almost as high as herself. As Hannah shot her first arrow straight into the centre of the target, Eramia tried to hold a serious face but joked,

'My father may take you away from being my servant and have you enlisted in his army!'

'Stop trying to make me laugh,' said Hannah, already lining up her next shot. 'At least lose with dignity.'

Eramia laughed as a second arrow embedded itself in the centre ring. When Hannah picked up the third arrow, she knew Eramia would be watching closely. Hannah composed herself, took aim, and then closed her eyes before releasing the shot. After the faint whistle and thud she said with her eyes still shut,

'Did I get the centre?' She said all innocently, knowing she had done.

'Crael!' Eramia exclaimed, 'I have a Crael for a maid.'

Hannah turned and beamed, secretly loving those comments made by her mistress and taking them as a high honour.

Eramia hit the target all three times after Hannah but only once managed to place an arrow in the centre circle. Therefore, the two carried on talking, teasing, and firing arrows, both in their own mind hitting wild beasts or dragons, fighting wars, or imagining some other fantasy from one of their beloved stories and wild imaginations when in all honesty neither of the two young women had left the castle and gone far without an armed guard. They longed to roam across the vast swaths of the beautiful land of Greenhaven, an environment both majestic and unforgiving.

3

The Arrival at Castle Tanath

For two days and a night, Sebastian had walked the ancient trade trail through dark woods and rugged hills. On the crest of a small hill near Sebastian's destination, the trees thinned to reveal Tanath Castle below. It looked isolated by a full tide, appearing very secure within its sheltered bay. To the right of the castle the ground came directly off a mountain straight into the sea. From the water, the mountain, known as Sgurr Mhor, looked insurmountable with its shear rock face to the north side of the castle. However, when approaching Sgurr Mhor from the other side, out of the trees and meadows on its northern front, the assent was far less severe. On top was a guard station always operated by four men of the kings own army. If trouble loomed, they would raise the flag of Greenhaven, the sea breeze enabled a slight lift and flutter as it hung on the huge pole. The flag itself was ten foot by eighteen foot in size. The background of the flag was white with a sea-green shield placed in the centre. The shield bore the words, '*Seasaidh Sinn Ar Tir*,' translated from the ancient tongue as 'We Stand Our Ground,' and this was also in white. When the flags were new and carried by many into battle, it gave the army an almost angelic aura.

Sebastian breathed a sigh of relief when he noticed that nobody had hoisted the flag.

He thought to himself, *I still have time ... I still have time.*

Sebastian lifted his face to feel the remaining warmth of the setting sun as it moved across the little islands that formed the end of the bay to the south west of the castle. The islands themselves were a good defence. The islands were too small for anyone to inhabit and it was only safe to bring a ship through them a certain way, often through the narrowest stretches of water. Many an invader had ended their conquest on those islands, the jagged rocks dashing both ships and men alike as the rolling waves of the ocean broke upon them in their restlessness.

Sebastian descended the hill hoping to reach the castle by nightfall. Although in all reality the woods were no less safe during the day, the darkness of night only added fear to Sebastian's imagination making the journey even more unpleasant. Sebastian made his way down to the main road that led straight to the castle. Castle Tanath looked quite uninviting silhouetted against the pale blue sky of the remaining day. The odd yellow light from unseemly placed windows cast strange shadows over the short tract of water from the castle to the shore. Tanath Castle was built not only upon a rock, but also into and out of the same rock. From the front, the natural rock at differing heights slowly became crafted stone walls. The small island on which Tanath was constructed was not in itself overly large; it was longer than it was wide. From approaching the castle by land therefore, it appeared to be quite thin and narrow. This impression was reinforced to some degree by the fact that the fortress was also fairly tall. Almost at sea level, and not much bigger than a man, stood a small door behind the main gate. The gate was comprised of two stone pillars that were hewn out of the natural rock and strangely carved. The door, when entered, led to a small courtyard surrounded by high walls, with a single staircase leading up to the main courtyard. It served as a good defense in times of trouble. There were four stout towers on each corner of the outer wall and four thinner, but taller towers, on the walls of the main hall, which was on the centre of the rock and slightly risen. However, the taller towers were not built at the corners of the Great Hall, but into the middle of the walls, equidistant from the towers on the outer walls. The door into the Great Hall was through the bottom of the tower that faced the land and to the east.

When Sebastian reached the edge of the shore facing the castle, the tide was too high to cross on foot. There were soldiers posted on the land as sentries and these would signal to the castle guard by torch when anyone needed to cross. A man in a small boat would row across to collect any visitors.

'I have news for King Orran,' Sebastian said to the men who stood around a meager fire. They had watched this lonely figure approach along the open road towards them.

'Your name and your business, Sir,' a gruff voice replied over the burning cracking of the wood.

'My name is Sebastian, I am a Brother at the monastery of Ness, we were ...,' he quickly stopped. 'I have news for the King and I wish to speak to him.'

The soldiers often viewed the monks as eccentric characters, although they often regarded them as trustworthy too, and there was seriousness to Sebastian's tone and face on which the soldiers felt compelled to act. A moment or two passed.

'Help yourself to a drink,' the gruff voice said, 'we'll call the boat over, it will take a few minutes.'

Off went two of the soldiers carrying a torch. Sebastian ate and drank but refused to sit with the other men.

The King must be the first to hear this news, he thought to himself. He refused to be drawn into any conversations about his recent past for it may have spread panic among the people.

He stood under a pine tree and watched for the boat.

A faint glow appeared above the castle walls indicating to Sebastian that there was movement from within. Then a small light flickered at the base of the wall shedding random light and shadow upon what looked to Sebastian like two men. They got into a boat moored to the rocks and headed towards the small band of soldiers on the beach. The night was exceedingly still. The noise of the movement in the water grew louder as the little vessel drew nearer the shore. A short stocky man with a bald head was rowing the boat. At the other end of the boat facing Sebastian, sat a hooded figure. This person was dressed mainly in black, bar the dull silver of his light armour, which was covered for the most part by his cape.

Before the boat reached the land one of the soldiers shouted out into the night,

'This monk wishes to see the King; he comes with news from Ness.'

At this, the hooded figure raised his head ever so slightly. Sebastian could not tell, but he was convinced the hidden eyes were pointing firmly in his direction. The boat grounded on the sand and the mysterious figure got out and walked towards Sebastian, who was still lingering under the branches of the shoreline tree.

'My name is Sebastian and …'

The man stretched out his arm with his palm raised and brought it to his lips,

'Sssshhh, lower your voice friend,' said a deep voice out of the darkness, and moving next to Sebastian and in almost a whisper he continued, 'What news from Ness?'

Sebastian was not sure he should speak to this stranger, but he felt he had no choice.

'We were attacked,' Sebastian whispered back, 'I alone survived, the monastery was sacked, and it was the Men of the North and ...' Sebastian hardly breathed as he spoke.

'Who have you told?'

'No-one,' said Sebastian shaking his head, 'they only know I came from Ness,' he continued, looking towards the soldiers who stood huddled together staring in Sebastian's direction.

'Come with me, the King is expecting you.'

This saying puzzled Sebastian, 'How could the King possibly know I was coming?' he mumbled to himself.

The two men left the tree by the water's edge under the star filled night sky. If it were not for the fact that Sebastian was so tired, and perhaps because it was dark, he may just have noticed the breastplate of the man's armour. '*Seasaidh Sinn Ar Tir,*' was written upon a black shield. Only one man in Greenhaven owned that armour and Sebastian need not fear him, but as things stood, he was uneasy about rowing into the night with the little bald man and the man in black. The three men headed for Castle Tanath. No-one spoke a word, but the bald man starred at Sebastian with an expression that looked half like a smile and half like he was in pain.

The boat arrived at a narrow ledge that had been carved out of the rock just below and to the right of the castle door. When the bald man had tied the boat secure Sebastian said, 'thank you,' as he stepped onto the ledge.

'He cannot hear you,' said the man in black, 'he's deaf.'

Sebastian turned towards the man, still in the small boat, and with a smile bowed his head. The man just nodded and raised his hand in acknowledgement.

'We trust him more than most,' spoke the voice from under the hood, as the two men passed through the door into the small deep courtyard of Tanath Castle.

Sebastian lifted his head and looked up towards the castle and its towers. A number of torches were burning along the castle's passageways, these led from where they stood, up the stone staircase and onto the main courtyard. Once Dante had firmly shut the door behind them, he removed his hood and turned to Sebastian.

'Now we can talk more freely, voices carry across the still water.'

Sebastian half nodded in response but did not really hear what the man said, as he stood there staring at him. He had never seen him before but he recognized him from the stories he had heard. The man had straight black hair which semi covered his eyes at the front but was longer at the back. A thick black beard covered his face. His black eyebrows topped his piercing blue eyes; eyes so clear and focused Sebastian avoided eye contact but for short glances. Into the left eyebrow and across the side of his head a scar was easily noticeable and the black of his hair and the blue of his eyes were made all the more prominent by the paleness of his skin.

'My name,' he said, 'is Dante.'

Sebastian nodded again.

'I protect King Orran at all times, and I'm captain of the guard,' Dante added. 'You bring unwelcome news to troubled times, but the King is looking forward to meeting you, for Ninian speaks highly of you.'

After saying this Dante turned around and made his way up the staircase and Sebastian followed, his mind inundated with stories of his new acquaintance. Dante was a man of war and his reputation was known throughout Greenhaven and the kingdoms roundabout. Although the castle had known peace for many years, the borders were rife with renegade leaders trying to make for themselves a name. The battlefield was a second home to Dante. It was not that he enjoyed war, nor the fact that he was very good at it, it was more a case of a man consumed with the seriousness of his service to the King, and his service brought him joy. He once held an outpost single-handedly against one hundred and forty men, fighting from noon to dusk until his sword became almost an extension of his arm and he had to peal his hand from the sword when all his enemies were dead.

The people of Greenhaven tell many stories about Dante, but not all of them are true. However, he did overcome a pack a wolves one snowy day when the King's hunting party became temporarily the prey. Yet for all his eyes had seen and his hand had done in battle, his heart was not yet hard, but he did not suffer fools, and romance and women were mainly foreign to him. Dante was one of the most self-controlled men not living in a monastery the King had ever known.

Sebastian and Dante had passed over the main courtyard, above which a stag had been carved into the stone. They walked up a number of stairs, through multiple doors, and along various corridors. Sebastian followed without noticing where he was going, his mind full of stories of war. Dante stopped outside the door of a room at the top and towards the back of the castle.

'Please,' Dante said, beckoning him in. 'I will have someone bring you some warm water to wash. There is food on the table already.'

Sebastian turned to look at the plate of cold meat, bread and fruit, close to the open glowing fire. Dante saw the back of his head and added,

'And perhaps someone to look at your wound?'

Sebastian turned to Dante and nodded, with an anxious look on his face.

'You'll live,' said Dante, 'I know a death wound when I see I one.' He then turned and left the room, his big heavy strides echoing down the empty corridor. 'The King will meet with you tonight,' he shouted back towards Sebastian, who had sat down by the fire and was eating an apple.

The warmth, wine and food, soon helped Sebastian fall fast asleep. The gentle soul sat with his arms folded, head forward and legs outstretched in front of him. He did not intend to fall asleep; he did not even consciously feel tired, but the wounded monk alone in his quiet room, slept.

4

Forbidden Pleasures of Uninvited Eyes

Eramia sat by the stain glass window in her room reading by candlelight.

'Eramia,' said a young female voice. There was repeated knocking on Eramia's door. 'Eramia, Eramia.'

'What has got you so excited Hannah?' Eramia replied as the door of her room flung open making the candlelight flicker in frenzy.

Hannah stuck her head round the doorway,

'Guess what I saw?'

'How could I possibly know?' said Eramia half concentrating on finishing her paragraph in her book.

'I saw Dante row out to pick up a man from the shore, it turns out he's a monk, I think he said he was from Ness? Anyway, he has some sort of nasty wound and he is meeting with your father tonight with some of the others and ...'

'Slow down,' said Eramia, trying to process the torrent of information that greeted her quite unexpectedly, 'we are in no hurry.'

'But that's just it,' said Hannah interrupting, 'The monk is meeting with your father soon. If we go to the Great Hall we will be able to listen in.'

Eramia looked at Hannah with her head to the side and her eyebrows raised, the expression she often found herself using with Hannah as if to say, *I do not think we should be doing this.* Nevertheless, like a cat, her curiosity often got the better of her.

Who was this wounded monk? Why is he here at this time? Why did Dante go to meet him? she thought among a host of other silent questions.

Hannah could see Eramia thinking and speculating as she stood at the door smiling and biting her bottom lip. Eramia sighed and stood up.

'Why do I know we should not be doing this?'

'It's an adventure,' Hannah replied, 'well, strictly speaking, someone else's adventure!'

'Perhaps one *we* shouldn't be listening in on!' Eramia exclaimed as Hannah took her hand and led her towards the Great Hall.

In order not to be seen, Hannah led Eramia through servant's passages as they weaved their way along the dimly lit corridors. The Great Hall was where the King and his advisors settled the business of the kingdom. It was a large room with a high ceiling and huge beams. There were four huge pillars on which the roof of the Great Hall rested. In the middle of the room were twelve stone throne-like chairs with seats of oak and dark green cushions. In the centre of the circle was a rectangular slab of rock, intricately carved on all four sides with scenes of the sea, horses and warriors. It had a smooth polished surface on top and many a map, plan, or proposal had been laid out upon its cold surface. At the western end of the hall, there stood latticed panels of wood. The servants would normally wait here until called upon when the King held a royal function. It was here that Eramia and Hannah found themselves standing when they heard footsteps approaching from the main door of the hall.

The door, made of solid oak, was opened by one of the guards and cracked as it turned on its hinges. In strode Ninian carrying a bundle of scrolls and papers, followed by Orran trying to keep up behind. Orran walked up and down a lot but every now and then had to stop to lean on a chair or against a pillar. He looked anxious,

'If what he says is true we will need to act sooner than we thought,' Orran said, speaking of Sebastian and his news. Then turning to Ninian he lowered his voice, 'If this is the Sebastian you know, how well can I trust him?'

'If it is Sebastian, you will find few better men to serve you, my Lord,' Ninian replied.

Orran nodded as he walked.

'He is a faithful man of God ... and skilful with a sword,' Ninian added.

Both men looked up and turned towards the door as it opened again. In came Dante, he had a tense expression on his face and he was followed by Sebastian who wore a new habit.

Eramia had been wondering what type of man this Sebastian would be, '*A monk and a warrior?*' she thought. When he walked into the hall and she saw that youthful rugged face with his dark brown hair falling into his innocent eyes, all time seemed to stop and her heart melted within her. Eramia fixed her eyes on Sebastian as she stared through the lattice, she could no longer hear the noise of the others speaking. She stared with so great a longing she raised her hand to her stomach and felt physically faint. That moment could have lasted forever and Eramia would have failed to notice any time had passed.

'Ninian!' Sebastian cried, as relief at seeing an old friend became evident across his face.

'Sebastian son,' Ninian began, going to greet him with a kiss, 'O Sebastian how I wish we met under more pleasant circumstances,' he sighed, embracing him with both arms.

Sebastian had learned under Ninian when he studied for the ministry and just before leaving for Ness. Ninian was dearer to him than his family.

Eramia had failed to notice Hannah watching her, seeing her so entranced by this holy warrior but she loved the feeling this gave her inside. However, Eramia could not pull her eyes away, for here before her was the man of all her daydreams and imagined adventures, the man who trusted in God like herself and yet was valiant in battle. Having never spoken a word to him or even seen him before, Eramia was besotted with the visitor that stood before her father. Eramia wanted him to herself. He did not know she existed.

As Sebastian recounted the events on the Island of Ness to Orran, Ninian and Dante, Eramia was captivated. She heard him speak, or more accurately, listened to him speak, for her concentration was firmly fixed on just beholding his appearance. Eramia loved all that she saw, for although she was in a room with five other people, she saw only Sebastian. Hannah touched her arm and Eramia reached out and placed her hand on Hannah's, but never took her gaze off Sebastian. Eramia held Hannah's hand firmly. Finally, turning towards her friend, Eramia smiled, her face was full of wonder and expectation.

The reasons for Sebastian traveling to Castle Tanath and the meeting that he attended that evening all seemed of little consequence now. All that presently mattered to Eramia she found sitting across the Great Hall in that unexpected visitor, that holy stranger, that wounded monk. Hannah however, gave greater heed and attention to the discourse of the four men unfolding in the midst of the circle of stone chairs.

When Sebastian had told the King of all that had happened in Ness, he asked the king how he knew he was coming. Orran looked across to Dante and reluctantly nodded. Dante rose and took one of Ninian's scrolls that he unrolled to reveal a map of the coast of Greenhaven upon the central stone.

'A number of my men had sighted ships about here,' pointing to the sea at the North of the kingdom. 'They were quite far out at first and they thought they were possibly merchant ships heading for the Summer Isles. Since then, sightings increased quite rapidly over a short period, so I went up to see if I could catch a glimpse of them for myself. Before I even reached the Grey Pillar on the northern peninsula I met one of my Frontier Riders who told me that attacks had begun along the coastal fringe and the ships carried the Men of the North. They were picking off easy targets at first, places of isolation and monasteries for the gold. On turning back to Tanath, I hugged the coast checking for danger. From the mountain above Ness, I saw it being attacked and burned. There were about twenty ships following the one that attacked you at the monastery. I also saw a single man leaving by boat and heading for the mainland, which it turns out was you,' said Dante looking at Sebastian. 'I described your appearance to Ninian and he suggested it may be you, given there were only three younger men residing on the island.'

Sebastian sat there piecing all the parts together.

'If it's the same people who raided Ness as it was further north,' Dante continued, 'we will *need* to muster the Craels for war.'

He said this placing his fingers over the handle of his sword. Sebastian looked at Ninian. Ninian sighed and stared blankly in front of himself. Orran gripped both arms of his chair and looked up at the roof as if hoping for a divine finger to write out what needed to be done on the cold walls of the hall.

Hannah turned to Eramia with wide eyes and an expression of shock, *war*, she mouthed, with a look of disbelief. It took a few seconds for the reality of a possible war to dawn on Eramia; her mind was still on Sebastian. The smile dropped off her face like lightening falling from the sky. She caught a glimpse of Hannah's expression; full of disbelief but revealing no fear. She then turned and gazed upon Sebastian's face, which looked exceptionally calm considering the proposal by Dante. Her dreams not long born were shattered into innumerable pieces. War alone would have caused her to weep, but the added fact that she may never get to know this man she had fallen in love with made her feel hollow. Her large brown eyes released a tear that slid effortlessly down her pale cheek, finding a home on her bottom lip.

Eramia turned away from Hannah and Sebastian and lowered her head, causing her rich brown locks to cover her face, trying to mask her tears. Eramia went to wipe away the trail of the tears, and as her delicate hand stretched out of her velvet sleeve, the silver bracelet on her wrist no longer remained hidden. Unknown to Eramia, the silver of her bracelet reflected with a dullish flicker from the torches burning on the sides of the massive pillars. Sebastian caught its movement out of the corner of his eye. As Orran, Dante and Ninian, were still in conversation and making strategies, he subtly moved his vision across to the wooden lattice lying mainly in the shadows, behind Dante and Orran to where his eye was drawn.

Eramia, wiping away her tears, wanted to leave and go back to her room.

I knew we should not have come, Eramia thought to herself, *it would have been better never to see Sebastian, than to have seen him, and loose him before getting to know him, let alone to now worry about war.* Eramia turned to look at him one last time. With this last lingering look of desire, she found him looking straight back at her from across the Great Hall. Eramia stopped, and staring into Sebastian's eyes, she saw all that she wanted in a man - his stare was noble, not intrusive, but accepting. Sebastian was as eager as Eramia not to end this most intimate of unexpected moments of beauty. For in her eyes he sensed tenderness and compassion, the very things he now sought in life. Eramia was momentarily unaware of Hannah tugging at her sleeve to depart, and as for Sebastian, he was oblivious to the present plans unfolding under the roof of the Great Hall.

As Eramia was dragged to her feet and led away by the hand back to her room she kept her eyes firmly fixed on Sebastian's gaze. Only the lattice separated these two young people from the unhindered pleasure of beholding the other, until Eramia slipped through a doorway into the darkness, her purple dress was the last glimpse of Eramia Sebastian was to have that evening. Oh, but what longing immediately rose in his heart to see her again. For in that woman, even in half-light, he saw untainted beauty, the beauty of a woman in perfect form. He knew in his heart he was feeling only physical attraction but it was a feeling he was pleased to pursue. Never before had any woman caused such stirrings in his heart. Up until now, he was glad about this, for being a monk in those days meant he had made a vow of celibacy and he never made a vow lightly. He knew he would never be able to marry this beauty in purple forever imprinted on his mind's eye, but his heart burned within him to see her.

To serve in her presence, he thought, *would surely bring enough pleasure.*

'Sebastian … Sebastian?' Ninian said, what are your thoughts on the matter? After all, it is you who have fought them once already.'

Sebastian could not recall the last few minutes of the three men's conversation, but the eyes of all three were upon him and were looking expectantly for an answer. He struggled to think of something to say but briefly remembering Ness he turned to Orran and said,

'I think war is upon us and you need to take action to save the lives of others.'

'Then let them see what it is to fight a Crael!' Orran said turning to Dante. 'Send out riders and gather the knights to Tanath. Prepare the men for war and we shall indeed stand our ground.'

Dante left swiftly in the remaining silence of the Great Hall.

'Sebastian, God saved you for the sake of our protection, but now you need to get some rest. We may need your sword again before too long,' Orran added to Sebastian's dismay.

Should I tell them about my vow never to fight again? Sebastian thought as he got up slowly to leave, but no words passed his lips.

'You and I must make further plans this night my old friend,' Orran said to Ninian.

'And lets hope they are not quite the last plans we make together,' replied Ninian, looking anxiously across at his king.

Orran and Ninian talked into the early hours of the morning about all that they needed to do, how they were going to protect Tanath's ancient walls. Dante sent out his Frontier Riders to raise the alarm and gather the Craels for war. Sebastian lay on his bed. After all that had happened all he could think about was Eramia, she was sweet medicine in helping to remove the image of his friend's bloody face. He did not even know her name, but her image in his head was as clear as running water and as he slept, he sought her in his dreams.

5

Farewell My Child

As the grey light of dawn first interrupted the darkness of the night, Sebastian made his way back to the Great Hall.

What will be my part in this war? He said to himself as he looked at the huge doors of the hall in front of him, victorious warriors depicted in its decoration.

Part of him was hoping that his contribution was almost over, but for that he barely dared to hope, for deep down in his heart he knew his whole life's experience had led him to this point. This gave him both a measure of peace and a mass of anxiety, realizing that this war may well lead him to his grave. As he pushed open the two wooden doors, there was Ninian and Orran speaking with Dante, as if they were reasoning with him, or as Sebastian first thought, convincing him of something. As he entered the hall, however, the monk, the soldier, and the King, all stopped talking and turned towards him. Sebastian mustered a half smile, being at a loss for a correct response at their unwanted attention.

'A few hours sleep, but hopefully good ones,' croaked Ninian, his voice becoming frailer due to the previous night's discussions.

'I had good dreams,' Sebastian replied, noting that whatever the three men had been talking about before he entered the room, had left Dante with a furious expression on his face.

Sebastian looked towards the wooden lattice at the far end of the room and was disappointed that the shadows there were *just* shadows. Nevertheless, before he had time to be downcast about the mysterious woman's absence, Orran broke into the course of his thoughts.

'Sebastian, I would like you to meet someone who is very precious to me, someone very dear to my heart.'

Sebastian lifted his eyes towards Orran, who stretched out his right arm towards the window. There, in all the beauty of the morning sat Eramia on the stone windowsill, with Hannah standing by her side. Sebastian gazed in amazement. The soft morning light emanated through the coloured glass of the window, which had the image of a tree bearing many fruits, the light adding a sense of majesty to one who was alone so naturally delightful to the eye.

'This is Eramia, my daughter. My only child and heir to my throne,' Orran continued.

Sebastian walked towards her and as he approached, she stood up from sitting on the window's ledge. Her hair was coloured by the light of the window so that she had tints of green, blue, and orange, down her long loose ponytail. She was roughly Sebastian's height, but the length of her hair and dress made Sebastian think she was taller. Eramia wore a sapphire blue dress, which had embroidered silver around the low neckline and bands of silver around her upper arms. The remainder of the sleeves consisted of fine white linen and hung very low from her arms, these she held together across her waist. As Sebastian drew near, Eramia held out her hand, but failed to find any appropriate words with which to greet him. Sebastian gently took her hand in his and held it tenderly.

'It is an honour to meet you, my Lady,' he said looking intently into her eyes, before he bowed before her and lovingly kissed her hand. He wished to hold it longer and kiss it far more than once. Sebastian had his back to the three other men at this point, but they could all see Eramia's face and they were indeed looking. Wishing to hide her true feelings for Sebastian, Eramia put on an austere face and looking down upon him as he bowed, she said,

'I hear you serve my father well, man of God. You are most welcome at this time of need, you and your sword.'

Sebastian lifted his head and looked her straight in the eye.

'I hope I may serve you as faithfully, if the need ever arise, my Lady,' he said, slowly releasing her hand.

Eramia gave a slight bow of the head in gratitude, 'And this is Hannah, my maid and faithful friend.'

Sebastian smiled at Hannah, who curtseyed in return.

'May you indeed serve her as faithfully as you have me,' Orran said, 'for the hour has now come, and the need has now arisen, and once again, your timing is impeccable.'

Sebastian turned and looked at Orran, along with both Eramia and Hannah.

'During our discussions last night, Ninian suggested, and we both agreed, on this one thing. It will not be safe for you here, Eramia, in the days that are coming upon us. I am sending you away Eramia … until the danger facing Tanath has passed,' Orran said uncompromisingly.

Eramia looked horrified.

'Leave? … Leave? … To go where? Tanath is my home and if I am to face any danger I will face it here,' she hastily stated.

'I have made up my mind, and I did not make this choice lightly,' Orran said, raising his voice substantially.

'I will not leave, I will not, I will be safer here,' Eramia protested.

Orran looked at her sternly but with a father's eyes full of love for his child.

'You are heir to my throne and this kingdom. This place will not be safe for you. If I die, the people need a ruler who will be fair and just, this shall be your calling, and then you can choose to stay through wars and famines if you desire. Dante and Sebastian will journey with you, and Hannah, of course. You will go inland and stay there until it is safe for you to return.'

Sebastian looked shocked at this suggestion, but was overwhelmingly pleased with the plan, *Away from trouble and in the service of Eramia*, he thought. Dante began arguing against the plan, which was why he looked so angry when Sebastian first walked into the Great Hall.

'Who will lead the men if not their captain?' He snapped.

'Valdar will take the Craels to war, he is more than able,' said Orran, in a tone which was meant to remind Dante who was King.

Hannah could not quite believe she was embarking on a real adventure, and the prospect silently shook her brave confidence. Eramia looked at her father, her eyes full of sorrow, but she did not weep because she was too angry.

'*Ehm L'Anya*,' Orran said softly to her, and he took her hands in his own and held them close to his chest. For this was Eramia's name in the ancient language of Greenhaven, and Orran rarely used it because he loved it so much, and dared not make it ordinary, nor common.

'Unwanted times encroach upon us my dear,' Orran said to Eramia. 'And I must do what is best for the people God has entrusted to my care. The people love you Eramia, and although I wish you were by my side in my darkest hour of need, I cannot, nor will I, put my own desires above their needs, and they *need* you alive and safe.'

Eramia sensed a great anguish in her father's voice, and with her eyes closed, she reluctantly nodded in agreement. The King and his daughter stood in the morning light clasping each other's hands. Eramia rested her head on her father's chest; Orran lifted his head and eyes to heaven once more,

Protect her Lord, he prayed to himself. *If all else falls, keep her under the shadow of your wings.*

'You shouldn't leave it too long before you set off either,' Ninian added wisely and glancing at Dante.

Eramia turned to Hannah, and they both began to leave the Great Hall. Eramia looked behind at her father – he was so very pleased with his daughter, and managed to smile as she left.

'Take only what you need,' Dante said, still evidently annoyed, 'We travel light and fast. I will meet you at the gate in one hour.'

Sebastian also went to leave the hall and pack but Orran grabbed his arm; his countenance had changed and he seemed incredibly serious.

'Serve her well, Sebastian … even with your life!' Orran strengthened the grip on Sebastian's arm. 'Ninian chose you because as a man of God you may comfort her, and as one who carries a sword, you may also provide her with protection.

'I will do both,' Sebastian replied immediately, full of honour.

'I hope you are not as quick to break your vow, as you are to make it,' Dante said to Sebastian privately, as he walked passed and left the hall.

Sebastian suddenly remembered his vow never to kill again, and if he was honest with himself, he regretted he had made it. He feared within his heart that there would come a point in his life where he would break that vow. As Dante passed Ninian on his way out Sebastian noticed that his old friend pushed something into Dante's hand, which Dante then kept concealed.

'Be sure to take a little wine with you,' said Ninian, 'the cheering powers of a good wine go a long way in making a hard journey far less unpleasant.'

'Pray for me Ninian,' Sebastian said, with his vow in mind.

'I've never stopped!' Ninian said, with the voice of an old man, as he and Orran disappeared into the castle's labyrinth of corridors.

Sebastian hurried back to his room to gather the few things he had brought with him from Ness. He packed what fruit and cold meat he previously left on the wooden plate in his room, then taking Ninian's advice, emptied the jug of red wine into a wineskin. Amidst all the rushing around, he managed to catch a glimpse of the sun reflecting off the deep blue sea, which caused him to stop. He marveled at its magnificence, and for some reason stopped rushing about, focusing instead on his calling in life.

'These events have come upon me Father, I did not look for them, nor choose them, but since I find myself in them it must be part of your will for my life. Therefore, provide me with the strength to do your will, to be faithful O Lord, in both love and service … if the two can ever be separated? He prayed.

Sebastian was just about to head for the front gate and meet the others when on turning away from the window he saw his sword leaning against the wall. Numerous thoughts flashed across his mind. Among them, his oath to Orran to protect Eramia, plus the doubting remarks from Dante regarding his character, and Rastko's bloody face staring right at him. His breathing became heavy,

What use will I be without it? He said to himself, *I have to take it*, he said, thinking of his word to Orran and the possibility of protecting Eramia, *I'll just try not to use it.*

This last persuasion even failed to sound reasonable to Sebastian but he was trying hard to ease his conscience but in the end, he angrily picked it up and strapped it to his side. He quickly closed the door to his room behind him so as not to encourage indecision and then made his way down to the main gate.

Unlike Sebastian, who had few possessions, Eramia and Hannah were facing multiple dilemmas regarding what to take, what to leave behind, and what they would and would not need. They choose their hunting clothes to ride in, but each took an extra two changes of clothes for warmth or incase they got wet. Eramia had a pair of long brown leather boots that she loved. On the outside of each leg there were wild horses fashioned into the leather. She wore them under a dark brown dress, which had subtle gold lace embroidered on the front and down to the waist. Around the sleeves and collar, a slim layer of fox fur provided both extravagance and warmth. Hannah wore a dark green dress, which was almost black in certain lights. It matched her riding boots, and the intricately woven shawl she carried on her shoulders, of a green, red, and dark blue tartan. Eramia also took the hooded cloak her father had given her when her mother died. It was double sided and could be worn either way round. One side was a rich ivy green colour and the reverse was deep purple. Hannah took a bow and a sheath of arrows, and urged Eramia to do the same but she refused. The only weapon Eramia carried was a small knife with a handle of antler, which she kept in the inside of her right boot.

Hannah was personally excited about the prospect of undertaking such an adventure but was afraid to share her enthusiasm with Eramia, who was clearly less enthralled with the whole situation. Eramia was too concerned with the future of her father and Castle Tanath at this moment in time.

'Now you can find out all you desire about this Sebastian,' Hannah said, tentatively trying to take Eramia's mind off more depressing things.

Eramia gave a wry smile.

'Yes … yes, I guess you are right … why is it that opportunities for good things often flow out of times of great trial?' Eramia replied.

Hannah did not answer; in her own mind, her job was complete. Eramia was thinking once more about Sebastian and how gently and affectionately he had previously embraced her earlier that morning.

Could he love me in return? Eramia thought, *surely it is not possible that a monk could ever be with a woman in the way … the way I wish to be with him?*

Eramia argued with her reason and logic as the two young women left the safety of their rooms into an unknown future.

Dante was waiting at the gate already mounted on Fhad, his horse, when Sebastian joined him. Dante appeared to Sebastian to have stopped seething, but still looked along way off from entertaining light conversation. It would have come across to many that Dante was just plain rude but he genuinely desired the safety of the King and Castle Tanath. He thought he was of far more use to his men at Tanath, rather than being in the woods with *two maidens and a monk*, as he had come to call them in his own mind.

Sebastian looked at the other three horses Dante had taken with him, and just before he asked which horse he was to take, Dante said,

'The brown and white horses are Lady Eramia's and her maid's. Your horse is this one here,' pulling a large chestnut brown beast in front of Sebastian's view.

Sebastian stroked the horse's long brown nose and looked into its huge reflective eyes; he feed him some of his apple as he ran his other hand repeatedly through the fine mane. No sooner had he mounted his new traveling companion, when Eramia and Hannah accompanied with Orran and Ninian, appeared from under the small doorway onto the narrow stretch of land. The land was only accessible at low tide.

Ninian took Dante to one side and began talking to him. Dante's face changed considerably; he looked almost pleased and patted Ninian on the back. Then both men turned to look at Orran and their faces became sad again.

'Be all she needs you to be,' Orran said to Hannah fondly, for it was Orran who had suggested that Hannah should go with Eramia.

Orran turned to Eramia and she fell into her father's open arms, holding onto him very tightly.

'Do all things well,' he whispered in her ear, 'be ready to be queen,' he added barely audibly. 'O my dear daughter … and do not seek love where love itself cannot be given!'

Eramia looked at her father in surprise. Orran smiled kindly. Eramia turned to Sebastian who was looking up into the hills, then turned back to her father.

'I did not seek love, father,' she began, 'but love has sought out me.'

They embraced again before Orran helped Eramia onto her horse. Orran, however, found it hard to let go.

'You know that I love you?' He said to his daughter, 'I love you so very much.'

Eramia reached down and took her father's hand; she was puzzled at his behaviour for he was usually so demure when it came to expressing his own emotions. There was almost grief in his tone. Eramia thought this despite the fact that war was on its way to Greenhaven. Her father's words were heavy to bear.

'I know, I know ... I love you too,' she replied with a smile.

Ninian and Dante's faces were also incredibly solemn as they watched the King say farewell to his daughter.

Orran faced Dante, whose black hair shone in the sun.

'It is at this time that you do me and this kingdom your greatest service, my friend.'

'It is perhaps more service than choice,' Dante replied.

'Yet you still choose to serve?' added Ninian.

'I do,' Dante said, nodding and looking Orran straight in the eye, before digging his heels hard into Fhad and moving off down the slippery causeway.

Sebastian raised his hand to Ninian and Orran and set off behind Dante. Lady Eramia and Hannah were quick to follow his lead. Ninian headed back into the castle's walls but Orran remained, watching as the four figures reached the dry ground and set off at a faster pace.

The wilderness for a refuge? He thought, as he stood there wondering what would become of the four riders he could see fading into the cover of the trees and the advice he had accepted from Ninian.

Hope, he said to himself, *what a precious gift ... O Eramia!*

6
News from the East

The forest path was littered with the dappled light and shadow of the risen sun falling through the leaves of the slowly swaying trees. Dante always led the small company from the front and often a little ahead of the other three. At first, Sebastian tried to keep up with Dante, but that only created a greater distance between himself and Eramia. Knowing that Dante could well look after himself, Sebastian dropped behind to ride side by side with Eramia and Hannah.

'If you feel you ever need to stop or rest a while then please say my Lady,' Sebastian said to Eramia, 'for your safety and well being must come first.'

'I may be the daughter of the King and dwell in fine clothes and eat fine food, but do not mistake my privileges, or being a lady, for weakness sir.'

'I meant no offence your majesty,' Sebastian quickly replied, 'I just meant … well I was just trying to say … that … well, if you did need to stop then you only need to say.'

'Yes sir, I know,' said Eramia sharply.

Sebastian felt quite small by her tone and answer, and thought that whatever he was going to say next would be wrong or cause offence. After a few embarrassing moments of awkward silence, he thought he might try to catch up with Dante again. However, as he accelerated forward, he turned back to Eramia on his right and said,

'You can call me Sebastian; I will not think you less of a Lady for dropping the "sir",' and waited eagerly for a reply.

Instead of hearing any words however, there came the increased clapping of hooves until Eramia drew level to his side once more. She was, deep down, very pleased that Sebastian had not only made the effort to speak to her but to speak to her so freely. She found this was very rare among men. She loved Sebastian's youthful innocence, not only in her presence, which often caused the bravest of men to crumble due to her elegance, but also in the presence of Orran, Ninian and Dante. He never appeared to Eramia to be anything other than who he was, and this genuine character intrigued her.

Eramia turned to him this time, and although Sebastian could see she was looking at him, he tried to keep focusing forward, waiting for her to speak first. As strong as he tried to be, he could not resist the desire in his heart to meet her eye to eye. Their gaze met as he slowly turned his head towards her, but to his surprise, neither of them spoke a word. Yet there was no awkwardness or embarrassment, only a sharing in the other's silent company, an acceptance that brought them both an incredible joy.

Eramia and Sebastian found the journey to be very pleasing. The hours dwindled away unnoticed as they shared a kind word or smiled caringly along the way. They passed between woodland and mountainous moor and it was late in the afternoon when Eramia caught Sebastian's eye as he stared in awe at her. She smiled at him in return, and in that smile, all traces of sternness were swallowed up in the splendour and vibrancy of her youth. Her thick brown hair tumbled from her head framing in Sebastian's eye a picture that he would never forget; natural beauty crowned with a beautiful nature.

'Sebastian it is,' said Eramia softly, 'if you would do me the same favour and call me Eramia, at least while we stay out here in the wilderness, I would be very pleased.'

'You have a lovely name, it would be an honour,' Sebastian said bowing reverently.

The two smiled at each other once more as they continued riding side by side. Both of them knew how they felt towards the other and both knew in part how the other felt towards themselves. Neither dare say anything about how they felt however, a reflection of both their affections and youth. Eramia wondered if it was even possible or right to love a monk.

What could come of it? she kept thinking.

Sebastian was thinking if it would ever be appropriate to tell her how he felt, knowing he had vowed never to marry.

Would it be better if she never knew how much I loved her? He thought.

These questions abruptly ended when both Eramia and Sebastian had drawn in line with Dante, who they failed to notice had stopped in the middle of the road not far in front of them.

'What is it?' Sebastian asked him.

Dante sat on his horse not moving or making a sound, as if he was listening to something.

'Dante,' Sebastian said again.

'Horses are coming,' Dante replied as the others strained their ears to hear.

'How can you tell?' said Eramia.

'I can't hear anything,' added Hannah.

'Nor can I,' said Sebastian.

'Look at the puddle,' said Dante pointing to the side of the road.

Once they had all stopped straining to listen, they saw the ripples on the surface of the water and felt the faint vibration on the grassy path. Hannah drew up close to Eramia. Sebastian instinctively placed his hand on his sword and looked to Dante's lead. Dante however, sat calmly upon Fhad with both hands relaxed on the reins. He turned to Sebastian, and seeing his hand upon his sword, Dante smirked and began shaking his head.

'If I thought we were in danger we would not be standing in the middle of the path. It will be Valdar and the troops from the hill country on their way to Tanath. I have arranged to meet them on this path to gather news from the eastern front. I plan to take us on part of the road they have just travelled and they can tell us how safe the road east is these days.'

As the four companions sat in silence listening to the increasingly loud thuds of Valdar's approaching troops, Sebastian took the opportunity to look upon the one woman he had ever wanted. Eramia was the only female he had ever felt any desire for, and yet his vow of celibacy included Eramia and this troubled his conscience almost violently. Eramia fixed her eyes upon the crest of the gentle hill in the direction their path led, lined either side with tall fir trees.

'There,' she said, 'there they are,' pointing to the road's horizon.

White flags came into vision bearing the shield of Greenhaven. Dante leaned over to Eramia and Hannah.

'Veil your faces. It would not be good for the men to see the royalty of Tanath leaving what they are about to defend.'

Hannah wrapped her shawl about her face and Eramia placed the hood of her cape on and kept her head facing down. Both women moved in closer behind Sebastian and Dante, placing themselves between the two men on their right and the trees on their left.

Into view came the flags, then the poles, then the men, then the horses. Warrior after warrior ascended the horizon and galloped down like a stream of angels, all clad in full battle armour and adorned with the white banners of Greenhaven. On approaching the small group of travelers lingering in the middle of the road, the fierce looking man leading the troops raised his right hand and caused the potential charge to slow down. Dante rode a few strides in front of the three others, making sure no one would get too close to Eramia whom he was to protect, even though they were friends that approached.

Dante rarely trusted even his oldest of friends, for he knew his own heart and it scarcely pleased him. He stayed mounted on Fhad until the two men leading the army dismounted their horses and made their way towards him. Dante met the two men in the middle of the road, Dante a little away from Sebastian, Eramia and Hannah, and the two men a small distance from their troops. Valdar and Botherick were the names of the two men who met and talked with Dante.

Valdar removed his helmet revealing his long red hair and beard of matching colour and length. He was tall and well built, his eyes would flash with fire when he was angry and he moved around awkwardly and heavily, giving the appearance of a lion if it could walk on its hind legs. He was quite literally a beast of a man, and much to his soldier's dislike, his temper was easily kindled. Botherick on the other hand, was so short and stocky he was almost square. He had a shaved head, revealing not a few scars and cuts, and his stubble, along with his eyebrows, were short and thick. His appearance could be described in a single word: solid.

'It's been a long time,' Valdar growled to Dante as they met beneath the firs, 'and you are leaving again so soon?' he said, glancing across at Sebastian and the two young women.

'Not out of choice, my friend. The King wants me to escort these friends of his out to safer pastures,' he said, also looking back to Eramia and the others.

'Perhaps he thinks you're getting too old?' said Botherick smiling.

'I thought you were dead?' Dante replied dryly, to Valdar's amusement.

Then the three men laughed together, each familiar with the other's humour.

The two gatherings of people on either side of the three men strained to hear their discussion but to no avail. These three men of war talked among themselves, like any old friends who had worked the same trade for over twenty years, it is just that in their case, their trade was killing and the tools of their trade were swords.

'What news from the east? Dante asked Valdar.

'All is quiet. The border is well established and there has not been any major trouble since the Indimar dispute, but that was nearly two years ago.'

'Tell him about those cursed Ghindred meddlers though,' added Botherick.

Dante raised an eyebrow in quite eager anticipation at Botherick's remark and looked to Valdar for more information.

The Ghindred was a name given to a certain group of people who lived in the vast swaths of woodland stretching to the eastern frontier. They dwelt along the river deep in the valleys, the natural borderline between Greenhaven and the neighbouring Rundafeld, although the Ghindred dwelt along both sides of the river. They were not a race, nor a family, nor a nation, but a community drawn from all different backgrounds who sought an existence living as freely as they could from the woods that sustained them. In most people's eyes, they became the woods unofficial stewards or guardians because they depended on it so much. However, there were certain Ghindred who broke the law in their occasional extremity to defend the woods and this gave them a bad reputation with the people who lived in the towns around the edge of the forests. The Ghindred often attracted unfavourable types of character, like those people on the run from the law, but it was a harsh existence and those who failed to adapt, either quickly perished or moved back to the towns. The original Ghindred however, were a kind and very knowledgeable people, a core of which remained, but they were very wary of strangers. Because so many thieves and murderers headed for the woods and the cover of canopy and shadow, Valdar and Botherick classed all the Ghindred as enemies of Greenhaven and its laws. Dante knew better. His travels across the kingdom had often brought him into contact with the Ghindred. The woods were so vast, not even the Ghindred had explored every rock, hill, or tree. Over the years, the Ghindred had accepted Dante, to the extent that they helped him catch some of those wanted by the law who dwelt in their woods. Dante was drawn to their sense of loyalty to the land they had come to call their own.

'Hmmm …' Valdar murmured to himself with a look of concern on the rough skin of his face when Botherick had mentioned the Ghindred.

Dante looked at Valdar, who was quite obviously uneasy about the thoughts he was having, as if Valdar was trying to explain something to his own mind.

'Things have been seen in the eastern woods,' Valdar began, lowering his voice to barely a whisper. 'Shadows in the mist, whispers in the night of other men, strangers of a different kind glimpsed between the trees. The Ghindred have scarcely been seen of late, and the woods … Well, it seems foolish to say it … But the wood itself appears to have become still, even the deer no longer venture out to scavenge near the towns.'

Dante listened intently to every word. This news was of the utmost concern to him because it was to the eastern woods he was taking Eramia. Deep into the trees, a hard day's journey into the woods, there was a place where Dante himself used as a safe place to camp. He would lead them along the river, which the Ghindred of many generations had called the 'Halla Issla,' but was more commonly known as the 'Great Silver.' Dante wanted to take Eramia and the others far enough into the woods for them to go unnoticed, but not so far that they couldn't return to Tanath quickly if the need arose, as he once explained it to Eramia.

'Strange times indeed,' said Dante, when he realised his two brothers in arms stood staring at him while he remained in his thoughts. 'And time may not be on our side! The King awaits you,' Dante said to Valdar.

Valdar clenched his fist and raised it to his chest, Botherick followed.

'Peace be with you,' they both uttered.

'For Greenhaven,' Dante said, while his two friends remounted their horses.

As Dante got back on Fhad, he drew his sword and raised it to the sky. When Valdar, Botherick and the rest of the men started to pass by, Dante lifted up his voice,

'Ride fast, ride hard,' he said to the soldiers, with immense passion in his voice and the veins on his neck almost bursting. Then he shouted out, '*Seasaidh Sinn Ar Tir, Seasaidh Sinn Ar Tir, Seasaidh Sinn Ar Tir!*'

The troops all raised their clenched fists to their chests as they passed, two by two, before their captain. Dante remained on the verge of the path until all the fighting men had passed. He was a warrior from head to toe, from dusk until dawn, day in, day out, and he inspired the troops as they galloped off to Tanath invigorated, wanting not only to engage the Men of the North in battle, but to crush them and spill their blood on the rocks of Tanath. As the last of the men rode by, Dante lifted up his head and roared, partly in the shared enthusiasm of the army and partly out of anger that he was not going with them to Tanath.

Sebastian, Eramia and Hannah, all watched him and were struck with fear, but fear mingled with thankfulness, for they were thankful that he was on their side. Dante's eyes fell upon his three companion's staring gaze but no one said a word. Dante turned towards the east and moved off slowly on Fhad; his three companions still looking at each other speechless did not wait long before they began to follow his lead. Dusk soon turned to night, and the four almost vanished into the darkness, as they slowly moved along the path after the sun had set, against the cover of the trees.

7

Among the Strangers of the Woods

Sebastian sat with his back against a young pine tree, careful not to put his head against the trunk, which was still sore to touch. Through the gaps in the branches of the trees all around him, he could occasionally observe the moon, as the soft looking clouds gently fled from its presence. Even with the light of the moon, the woods at night held a dense blackness. Not far in front of him lay Eramia and Hannah, both asleep on the moss between the roots of a giant oak tree. He looked upon Eramia lovingly, even though she lay mainly hidden under her cloak. Sebastian actually held both the young women in high regard, for neither of them complained much about the harshness of the journey, compared to what they were used to,

But perhaps that may change in time, thought Sebastian, *especially if the days become weeks, or the clouds carry rain*, as he noticed the moon being engulfed in the passing clouds.

Dante had been sleeping close to Eramia last time Sebastian looked, but much to his annoyance he found Dante standing right next to him when he lowered his eyes from the skies.

'Dreaming is for sleepers,' Dante said to Sebastian.

'And do you never dream?' Sebastian replied.

'Too often,' said Dante, 'that is why I only take a little sleep.'

Sebastian thought he understood what Dante was saying, for since the attack on Ness, his own dreams had been strangely darker. He shuddered to think of the things Dante had seen in his lifetime, or the faces that called out to him in the still small hours. Dante could see that Sebastian had understood in part, and placing his hand upon Sebastian's shoulder, he said,

'Get some rest Sebastian, dawn is not far off, and we need to make it to the eastern woods well before nightfall. We do not want to have to stop in Rimbleton or any of the other towns if we can help it. Where there are eyes, there are also mouths, and questions that proceed from them! We will follow the old funeral trail; I know it well and that should bring us to the edge of the woods with at least partial cover.'

Sebastian nodded, but Dante could see his eyes were heavy and so left him to his sleep, propped up against the tree. After walking around their temporary camp, Dante came to the oak tree under which the King's daughter and her maid still lay sleeping. Dante leaned upon its rough bark and remained motionless for almost two hours, always watching, always listening. He was so still, that at one point, three deer walked passed him, no more than twenty feet away.

As the new day's sun stretched to reach into the morning's shadow, Eramia stirred. For a moment, she forgot where she was and sat up with a fright. The sight of Sebastian asleep in front of her and Hannah to her side was enough to remind her of the journey she had recently undertaken. Not to mention the tree root she felt digging into the top of her leg. Eramia sat still, resting on both hands, her arms outstretched behind her. She breathed in the morning's freshness and watched the damp leaves occasionally tumble onto the dew covered forest floor.

'Sufficient rest, my Lady?' spoke a quiet voice from behind.

Eramia turned suddenly as Dante moved out from against the tree.

'More than enough, thank you,' Eramia said softly, still not fully awake, but rising to her feet.

Eramia involuntarily shuddered as the cool morning air embraced her and she wrapped her cloak tightly round her body and placed the hood over her head, being thankful for its lush velvet touch. Eramia moved closer to Dante as Hannah and Sebastian remained asleep.

'Are you angry with me sir, because you are drawn away from the battle?' Eramia asked directly.

Dante smiled to himself, 'Angry?' he said. 'I am not angry with you, my Lady … No, not angry with you.'

'But it is because of me that you are here and not with your men at Tanath.'

'What you say is true, but I am not angry with you,' he said turning towards her.

'Then my father Orran, are you …'

But before she could finish her sentence Dante interrupted her, 'I am not angry with the King either, I have served him all my adult life.'

'Then what?' asked Eramia puzzled, 'I don't understand what is troubling you.'

'I have served your father many years now, but …' Dante broke his line of thought, and looking past Eramia into the shapeless blackness of the ground beneath the trees, quietly just stared.

'But what?' asked Eramia, pressing Dante for more information, as the silence grew uncomfortable, 'But what, Dante?'

Dante raised his hand, placed it on Eramia's cheek, and sighed.

'O child,' he said looking at her as though she were a little girl, 'your father I have served, but the day is coming when I will serve you instead … I hope I am as pleasing in your eyes as I am in your father's. If we had both stayed at

Tanath, I could have protected your father and shown to you how willing I would be, to even die for the one I serve.'

'You have always pleased me Dante,' Eramia said uneasily, looking innocently into his eyes as he looked down upon the ground. Eramia stared at him for a while but he would not raise his eyes to meet hers.

'It is time we were going,' Dante said, turning away from Eramia, who was left standing alone and a little intrigued.

It is almost as if he harbors feelings for me. Eramia thought to herself, *but why have I never noticed this before? And more to the point, he is twice my age.*

Dante, however, had no inclinations towards Eramia. He could clearly see she was very attractive, but his passions lay elsewhere. It was being a soldier he loved and serving Orran his King that pleased him, but what he had told Eramia was not wholly true. Dante could not tell her the truth just yet, as he had sworn an oath to Orran not to let Eramia aware of the burden he was to carry for as long as possible. The time Dante spent away from Tanath were days he could never regain, and Dante loved Orran like a brother; more than Valdar and Botherick, more than the troops and he too thought that Eramia was not quite ready to be the queen she would one day become. Not knowing he had unintentionally misled Eramia, he did not attempt to clear things up or straighten things out. The morning had begun unrepentantly early, and for Dante, had been regrettably eventful in a most unhelpful way.

Dante woke Sebastian and Hannah and prepared the horses to leave. Eramia stood against the great oak she had slept beneath, trying to rationalize her thoughts. Every time she tried to look Dante in the eye, he went out of his way to avoid her. None of the morning's misunderstandings hindered the day's journey however, as Dante was always in front of the other three, pushing them hard so they would make it to the woods by that afternoon. In fact, the old funeral path proved a very useful route to take as the four companions only passed a handful of people all day. Although they were tired, their spirits were in good form. Hannah and Eramia spent a lot of the day talking about what may be happening back at Tanath, and what the future and the eastern woods, had in store for them.

Sebastian remained quite noticeably silent all day. He had two reoccurring conundrums to juggle with, but all the pondering in the world was proving utterly useless. Sebastian's emotions varied from elation because of his love for Eramia, and disappointment that nothing could ever happen between them. These thoughts were quickly followed by guilt and he began to question his vow of chastity, which he was so sure was right when he made it. In fact, it had helped him focus on his service to God and in his life at the monastery. Back then, life inside the monastery was different in many respects. At Ness, Sebastian's knowledge of the Bible grew considerably; outside of Ness, he found his faith being tested with fire. *Now* he had seen Eramia, her undeniable elegance, his desires for her if he was honest, and all this seemingly reciprocated. The safety of Ness had fled away.

Whenever he managed to break free from this cycle of thoughts, another dilemma, worst than the first plagued him.

If the need arose, where I needed to use my sword to defend Eramia, would I kill again?

He tried to reassure himself that the need might never come, but the words of his vow; *never again will blood be spilt from my hand*, danced uncomfortably round in his mind. He would then look at Eramia, which made him feel increasingly guilty, as he contemplated not defending the woman he was forbidden to love. Outwardly, Sebastian appeared relatively relaxed, he was always polite and thoughtful of others, but inside he felt like his mind was being simultaneously ploughed in four different directions. He suddenly longed for the peace he once knew and took for granted on Ness with the fellowship of like-minded friends.

Dante was pleased with the progress they had made that day. They reached the edge of the eastern woods and had gone relatively unnoticed, avoided the towns, and more importantly, they had avoided trouble. The woods nevertheless, posed problems of their own. Dante's mind was troubled by the rumours of strange visitors, but for now, he welcomed the safety of the cover of the trees. The woods to the east were exceedingly old, and if the trees could talk, innumerable stories would be told about the people who have roamed within its boundaries. It was the kind of place that could change quite dramatically; dense, damp, tree filled areas would suddenly give way to bright airy clearings, with soft swaying grass of the most vibrant hues. Gentle rolling hills covered with trees would abruptly end at a steep rugged cliff, where small rivers forged their way through deep valleys, places so deep, even the sun had never managed to shed light into their cracks and crevices. It was a place where life could be heard all around you but rarely seen. The type of woods where there was always a pair of eyes set upon you at any given time.

The trees generally thinned out towards the tops of the mountains, but in the valleys and glens, trees, plants and other shrubs dominated everything. Under the canopies of the trees, centuries of falling leaves and gathering moss covered rock, stone and roots, leaving a multi-layered carpet of springy ground on which to walk. These conditions were ideal for people who want to move silently through the trees. A light mist would often be found in the early hours of the morning, breathing life into all it touched.

Running right through the entire woods was the Hala Issla; its watershed was near the centre of this expanse of wilderness. The river could be traced northwards out of the woods, then slightly more west into the sea, but it also continued in a southerly direction where it meet the sea once more, many miles away from its source. Near to its source, deep, narrow banks, unexpected falls, and a fast flowing current characterized the river. After its fight to carve its way out of the mountains in the woods, the Hala Issla became a much wider and gentler body of water.

Although Eramia and her companions entered the woods before the sun had set, it appeared in places as dark as night. The braches of the trees covered the sky above and drooped down towards them with various types of moss, like old men's beards, trailing from the branches. Sebastian looked around with great apprehension, his eyes still adjusting to the lesser light of his new surroundings.

'Dante, is this wise, bringing Lady Eramia to this kind of environment? Anything could happen to us and no one would know for days!' Sebastian complained, not overly content with the prospect of dwelling among the trees with who knows what sneaking around them. Sebastian was used to living by the sea; its sheer size and sense of infinity were much preferred, compared with the thickness of the forest he was presently experiencing.

'We are quite alone out here, aren't we?' Hannah added, not enjoying this aspect of her dreamt after adventure.

'Alone?' said Dante in a surprised tone. 'Oh, we're not alone … oh no, in these woods you can never be *entirely* alone.'

'Why do you say that?' Eramia asked, echoing the thoughts of both Hannah and Sebastian.

Dante turned towards them, 'I have friends here,' he said.

'But how will you find them?'

'That will not be a problem my Lady,' Dante said, 'they will find us, I'm sure.'

'What if the Ghindred find us before your friends do?' said Eramia in a very serious manner, recalling the outrageous tales she had heard from Valdar, Botherick and others, whenever they were mentioned at Tanath.

'Again, that need not concern you, my Lady,' he replied, 'for the Ghindred are the friends that I seek.'

'Sir, I must protest ...' Eramia began in amazement, before Dante cut her off quite sharply.

'You may protest all you like your majesty, but do not do it too hastily, for experience is to knowledge what stories are *not* to truth. Reserve your judgment, put away hearsay; the Ghindred serve a special purpose for your father's kingdom.'

Eramia saw the sincerity in Dante's face and held her tongue. She also was not quite sure what to say in reply; instead, she looked at Hannah with a troubled look on her face. Sebastian was both pleased and surprised with Dante's wisdom, and for the first time held out a possibility that he may even find a friend in Dante, although, what type of friend he still was not sure. Dante moved off slowly in the quietness of twilight between the ancient trees. A gentle breeze pushed its way through the tops of the trees causing the trunks to crack and creek, as if they protested to the involuntary dance. At first, these noises made Hannah and Eramia uneasy, but the further they ventured into the woods, the more accustomed they became to the songs the woods had been singing for centuries. Eramia and Hannah stayed close behind Dante; they did not want to meet his friends without him, especially not at night.

8

A Night for Revelations

A trickle of fresh water meandered down the rocks under the tall fir trees where Sebastian sat. The branches seemed to spread out only two thirds of the way up their slim, creaking trunks. The pine needles covering the floor helped minimize the noise from any movement, and since both Hannah and Eramia were tired, Dante decided to camp here for the night. Sebastian gathered some wood and twigs to light a fire, which he placed against a huge flat rock, near to where the water fell. The rock was about eleven foot in height at certain points. This was a good thing in Dante's eyes, as it covered the glow of the fire and smoke, and kept them sheltered from the wind. Dante made sure he had feed and watered the horses before joining the others around the fire. Hannah had already begun warming some of the cold beef they had taken from the castle.

'How are we doing with the supplies? Asked Eramia, in a very sensible tone.

'I don't think we took nearly enough,' Hannah replied. 'In fact, we seem to running quite short already,' she continued, not taking her eyes off the meat on the end of her stick, as the juices bubbled their way out and ran to the tips of her fingers.

'Perhaps Dante has some more hidden in his possessions,' Eramia suggested, almost talking to herself out loud, captivated by the flames as they danced around the cracking, glowing wood.

'No,' said Dante, as he approached the light of the fire from among the trees. 'From tomorrow we need to gather our own food. But don't let that trouble you my Lady,' he said reassuringly, 'there is an abundance of food to be found in the woods.'

'Do we get to hunt?' Hannah asked all exited, 'I have brought my bow,' she added, looking across to Eramia and smiling. 'It is becoming just like one of those adventures we have always talked about!'

Eramia was pleased for Hannah and glad that she was with her. Hannah's indomitable spirit for adventure would prove more than once to spill over into joyful optimism, turning a potential bleak situation into something containing hope.

'I've heard your knowledge of plants is rarely matched,' Eramia said to Dante, 'that should stand us in good stead.'

'You would be surprised at the amount of plants and insects that can provide you with a nutritious meal,' he commented.

Sebastian watched Hannah and Eramia's faces dramatically change expression, as they sat there looking at each other, wondering what creepy crawlies would be awaiting them for breakfast.

'Let's hope your skill with a bow is better than mine,' laughed Sebastian. 'If we linger by the river I should be able to catch us some fish,' he said, smiling along with Dante.

'The Hala Issla, or Great Silver as you may know it, contains an abundance of trout and salmon, and it's very close to where we shall camp. You see? Between us, we will be feasting every night! Dante said.

Nevertheless, Eramia and Hannah were not sure if Dante was being sarcastic.

'You seem to know the woods well my friend,' said Sebastian, implying he would like to know how he gained this knowledge of bush craft.

Dante, however, simply replied, 'Aye, I do,' and would not be pushed into adding any further information, despite the increasingly awkward silence that hung about the fire.

'How have you come to make friends with the Ghindred?' said Eramia, with a quizzed look on her face. 'Tell us, what are they like?'

'Thieves, murderers and the general lawless; doesn't everyone know what the Ghindred are like? Replied Dante, semi-mocking his future queen.

'We can know nothing about anything accept from what we hear from others,' Eramia said bluntly, 'and there's nearly always a little truth in generalizations.'

'Quite right, my Lady,' Dante said, sitting with his back against the stone and staring past her, over the fire, and into the trees behind, lost in some memories.

'Well?' she demanded.

'The first time I entered these woods was over eighteen years ago. I was hunting a man called Conrad, whom I had tracked through the Fisherfield Mountains for the attempted assassination of your father, Eramia, whilst we were on a hunting expedition. The man tried to take refuge in these very woods. Knowing there were others like him here, he thought he would be safe. Not long after I had entered the woods, I lost all hope of finding the man, and I was about to turn back and leave, when I heard a voice call out to me, "What is your business with the man you seek?" I tried to see if I could put a face to the voice, but I could see no one, so I called back, "who wants to know?" Then with the slightest of movement and minimum of noise, eight or nine men appeared out of the foliage. One of the older looking men approached me; he had a staff in his hand and a dagger on his side.

"We are the Ghindred," he said, "and I ask you again, what is your business with the man you seek?" I, too, had heard unfavourable rumours about these people, but not all the reports were bad. I noticed that apart from a few weapons for hunting, these men were in essence, unarmed. In fact, most of them, if I recall correctly, were only partially clothed, wearing skins and furs mixed with some normal items of clothing.'

Dante then paused, as if he was remembering things he had not thought of for years and years but were surprisingly vivid as he brought them to mind afresh.

'What did you say? Tell us,' Hannah said in anticipation. Sebastian and Eramia were equally enthralled by Dante's recollections, often smiling at each other as the story unfolded.

'Well,' he began, like a great story teller with an eager audience, 'I told them,' he said, 'I had nothing to lose. "I am in the service of the King," I said, "and the man I seek is wanted for attempting to kill him." The man, who spoke to me from the Ghindred, looked around at the others, who each nodded in turn. "Follow us," the man said, "we will help you if we can," and after he said this we moved off into the woods. Eventually we caught up with Conrad, but there was a struggle to arrest him; my blade met his throat, so we left him to the wolves. The man who spoke to me from the Ghindred was an elder of the woodland people, called Comasius, and he showed me wonderful hospitality as we later talked well into the night. I learnt that many centuries ago, the Ghindred elders met with King Thoran and a pact was established. The Ghindred could dwell in the eastern woods with almost autonomous rule, except they were under obligation to defend that area of Greenhaven against all foreign invasion, and they were to maintain the well being of the woods and the animals that dwelt there, providing enough beasts for the King to hunt and gather skins. To the true Ghindred this agreement stands and most do still honour the King and recognize his rule. On returning to Tanath and explaining everything to Orran, he wisely sent me straight back to find the Ghindred elders to say that King Orran is very much in favour of maintaining the ancient pact, once made with Thoran. From that point on, the Ghindred and I have worked closely together in the service of your father, Eramia.'

'Why is the agreement not public knowledge then?' Eramia asked, 'It would mean that the Ghindred are hated without a genuine cause, why would they put up with that reputation?'

Dante nodded in agreement with Eramia and continued, 'But this way, the King's enemies and the lawless wanderers flee to the Ghindred, only to be handed over to me or put to death by them. The people's hatred of them throughout the kingdom is the very cover they require for serving your father so effectively. They live as despised villains so the kingdom can be free of them. Their service is, and for centuries has been, sacrificial to the core. Although their reputation over the years had held well, how many people do you actually know who have been mistreated by the Ghindred?'

'I never knew …' mumbled Eramia, shocked.

Sebastian and Hannah sat there equally mystified by Dante's story, the mouth of one and the eyes of the other opened wide.

'When I later searched the library with your father, Ninian led us to a number of books detailing the Ghindred's history and standing within Greenhaven. All that Comasius said had been true. In fact, they were some of the original inhabitants of Greenhaven, and more than that, it is quite possible their blood still flows through the royal line!'

Eramia sat their speechless, lost in thought. Sebastian had compassion on her and looked at her lovingly.

'It all makes sense,' said Sebastian all of a sudden, 'the reason you brought us here, I mean. I did wonder why we were heading for these woods, given their reputation and vastness … but of course, where danger is falsely perceived, there is in fact safety. I was wrong to doubt you Dante, forgive me.'

Dante nodded again, but believed he had spoken far too much for one night, and so he let the fire speak into the night sky instead. The four of them sat there by the fire; no one spoke a word but there were a torrent of questions running through the minds of Sebastian, Eramia and Hannah.

The warmth of the fire, plus Eramia's over active imagination caused her to excuse herself from the others and seek some cooler air. She stood up and walked over to where the water fell from rock to rock, silver on black, the moon touching its surface as it played in the night. Eramia pulled back the long draping sleeves of her dress and gathered the cold water in both hands to wash her face. She would hold the water for as long as possible, until it was still enough to reflect the moon, and gazed in amazement at the moon held in her hands.

'A night for secrets and revelations it appears,' Sebastian said, approaching behind Eramia.

'Hmmm,' Eramia murmured, smiling politely and lifting her eyes to the host of stars shining above their heads.

There was silence between the monk and the princess but each tried to guess what the other was thinking, and who would be the first to speak, and what they would say. Eramia could hear the mild breeze brush the tops of the tall pines and watched as they swayed delicately below the stars. Various words ran through Sebastian's mind as he desperately tried to capture how he felt about Eramia and figure out why he had not yet spoken to her of his love. Looking down at the ground and not wanting to wait any longer, he opened his mouth and spoke whatever words came to him at that moment.

'It was you wasn't it? The night I met with your father in the Great Hall, it was you behind the lattice, wasn't it? Your eyes, you could never hide them nor disguise them. I've often been at a loss as to why you were there, and for the life of me, I still don't know why I didn't say anything at the time. I mean, you could have been anyone … My Lady, do not think me rude for what I am about to say, or too forward, for I am only a monk and do not pretend to be anything other, but permit me these few words … even if they make little sense or are fumbled.'

Eramia looked at Sebastian with her wide comforting eyes, which made him feel both a little bit foolish as well as a little encouraged.

'Well,' he said, taking a deep breath, 'although your mouth is silent, your eyes speak many words, and I'm hoping that what I am about to say will not come as much of a surprise to you … it's just that … well,' he sighed again. *Am I not a man*, he thought to himself, and confronted Eramia directly.

'I love you,' he said. 'Eramia, I think I'm in love with you,' Sebastian said again, but his face was not full of joy when he said it. 'I love you, but I cannot love you,' and with this he turned away, for the smile on the face of Eramia changed to an expression of despondency and he could not bear to see the change.

'A night for revelations indeed,' said Eramia slowly and quietly, touching Sebastian on his shoulder. She kept her hand on his shoulder as she walked in front of him, then took his rough hands in her smooth palms and placed her long feminine fingers between his weathered ones. She held Sebastian's hands tightly, and with her gaze, she lifted his head.

'Of all the wise men, noblemen, men of war and royalty who have sought my favour, I have never found love. Lust, power, riches; these were all there in abundance, but what are these things without love? I had almost lost all hope of finding my heart's desire – until the night a young warrior from Ness graced my father's court, a man of God who shows no partiality ... Sebastian, I loved you the moment I saw you, and yes, I love you still.'

Sebastian raised his head and his hands into the moonlit night, and would have cried out in despair but he knew he would have only drawn attention to himself from Dante and Hannah who still sat round the fire in silence, eating. It appeared to Eramia as if he railed against God, but she thought no less of him for that. Rather, she was pleased that she had found a man who was strong enough to be honest and open before God. Despite her declaration of affection for Sebastian, she knew why he felt as he did.

'I know we can never love each other, other than in word,' Eramia said. 'You have vowed never to marry – I understand that. I, as heir to the throne of Greenhaven, must marry and produce children. Our thoughts are one Sebastian. How do I love the one I love, who I cannot love?'

'Indeed,' sighed Sebastian, relieved Eramia felt the same, but crushing his heart further. 'And how can that ever be expressed? ... Or how can it endure? Or even be *denied*? Is there any heavier burden in life, than to be forbidden to know the love that is both willing to love and be loved?

'But to love at all is surely some kind of gift?' Eramia replied, convincing herself there was truth in her words, '... and to know that love reflected?'

'Will it not crush you? As it breaks my heart, I will not break my vow to God, but twice now I have vowed, and I stand an inch away from breaking both and …'

'Sebastian,' Eramia said softly, curtailing his impromptu speech. 'Sebastian, I do not want you to break your vows, your faithfulness to God is part of the reason I love you, and the more I know you, the more I know I was right to love you from the start. Then I loved you simply from what I saw of you, now I love you for who you are.'

'Then what is to be done?' interrupted Sebastian, 'Love and burn?'

'Let the burning of your heart be quenched by the knowledge that your love is not wasted, it is shared, no, more than that, accepted and returned, cherished and admired; let our forbidden love be forever known between us.' Eramia smiled and continued looking up at the stars, 'Let these stars be a witness to all that has been said tonight – not that we vow, rather that we know, despite who we are and what we can do, we love each other Sebastian. And let us pray it is enough to know we are loved, if it is the only love we can know.'

Eramia drew even closer to him, tenderly touching his face with her hands. The two, face to face, their hearts stolen by the other, saw in each other's eyes a love they would never be able to deny. Although it was a secret love, those who gave that love knew it quite freely. In the light of the moon and the cool of night, Eramia and Sebastian, loving each other deeply, sealed their love with a kiss. One kiss to seal a love never to be expressed again so openly, but a kiss so tender, so felt, and so perfect, as to satisfy their hearts, dispel all their fears, and to bind them in a union both were determined to keep.

Hannah put an end, temporarily, to their incurable passion.

'Did you hear it?' she said for a second time, 'I'm sure there's something out there, something moving, something watching us.'

Eramia and Sebastian loosened the hold each had on the other, and both looked down at Hannah as she made her way towards them. Now, the fact that Hannah, not to mention Dante, had witnessed their love concerned them hardly at all.

'Are you sure?' Sebastian asked Hannah, quite skeptically, seeing that Dante had not moved from the fire's side and knowing that if danger posed any real threat, Dante would be the first to know.

'I heard twigs snapping, I'm sure of it, and I thought … well I thought I saw something moving in the darkness over there, but, but …'

'Ssssh,' Eramia said, motioning with her hands for Hannah to be quite, 'lets stay together and close to Dante just in case.'

Sebastian took Eramia by the hand once more and led her off the rocks back to the fire and Dante, who now sat with his back to the woods and whatever may be lurking out there. As the three of them hurried to the fire, their eyes lay keenly on the dense blackness of the forest at the edge of the clearing. None of them could say for sure if anything dangerous was out there, but Dante's next words did nothing to comfort them or the situation. Dante rose to his feet as the others stood around him asking questions.

'I told you he woods are full of life … and yes, there are eyes set upon us even now,' Dante said quietly.

'How do you know?' Eramia replied, 'Are we in danger? What shall we do?'

'I told you,' Hannah added, over Eramia's questions.

Sebastian's hand instinctively lowered nearer to his sword, and he moved in between Eramia and the woods but at the same time, he had learnt to trust Dante and he looked to him before taking any action.

Unhesitant youth, Dante said to himself, before turning his attention to the others, 'slow to realize, quick to react.'

Dante looked past them into the trees, still shaking his head, he lifted his voice and raised his hands, 'Come,' he shouted, 'make yourselves known.'

Hannah and Eramia looked at each other horrified but quickly turned back to face whatever was going to approach them from the trees. Their curiosity conquered their fears. Sebastian did not move but his eyes were peeled and set like steel, his ears pricked back to capture any noise. Then as if the trees themselves moved, the darkness took shape until the forms of men became visible against the mass of trees. There they stood nine figures in the night. Dante turned once more to Eramia, 'The Ghindred, my Lady.'

Hannah's eyes grew wide, trying to take in as much as possible; she even smiled at the mention of their name.

'Real adventure,' she thought.

Eramia looked uncharacteristically brave. Sebastian remained unmoved.

9

The Men of War Take Council

When Valdar reached the beach before Castle Tanath, the first thing he did was look to Sgurr Mhor. He sat on his horse as the sea breeze refreshed his face and moved the horse's mane like waves. The flag of the guard station blew clearly by the western shore. Valdar turned back to address his troops and caught Botherick's eye, set in his grim looking face, for they both knew that war would be upon them soon.

'Men of Greenhaven,' shouted Valdar, as he moved slowly among his fellow warriors, 'the day to be all that we have trained to become will soon greet us, and it will be a violent day, a bloody day, a day of death as these beasts of the north come to seek our destruction. Let us fight with honour and immense courage, so that Tanath may stand, so that Orran may still reign and so that we will not be ashamed to be called men.'

A loud cheer rumbled into the sky as the soldiers lifted their voices and swords, their commander's eyes flashed with fire and eagerness to lay these invaders to waste.

'Tonight we camp here,' Valdar said to Botherick, 'and we'll move them fully armed into the castle tomorrow morning. The two of us will go over and meet with the King now.'

'Very well,' said Botherick, as he moved off and ordered the men to make camp and prepare for the morning.

As Valdar watched his men start organizing the camp, he wondered how many had seen a large-scale war before, and how many would perhaps only see one once.

This is it, he thought to himself, *the war I have always dreamed of and wanted, but now that it's here …*

'Valdar,' Botherick said again, looking at him as if he shared his thoughts, 'The boat is ready, let's go.'

Valdar exhaled a long heavy breath and made his way to the green boat looking up at the castle as he went. He was proud to see Tanath, its towers tall and firm, and the white flags of Greenhaven floating from its turrets.

'We shall stand our ground,' he said, not realizing he actually said it out loud.

'Aye,' replied Botherick, which took Valdar by surprise, 'and if we ourselves don't, Tanath will!'

This met with Valdar's approval, as he sat in the boat grinning wryly. Both of them were pleased to see the castle in a state of business, even though it was busy with soldiers preparing for the worst. Soldiers were positioned all along the defences, which ran the entire length of the castle's main walls.

Those who were in Tanath met Valdar and Botherick with a hero's welcome and they spent a little time strengthening the men with words of courage and comfort before being led by Narses into the Great Hall to sit with Orran.

Narses was in charge of the castle's defenses under Dante. He was a thin man, with a large crooked nose and drawn features. His eyes were deeply set and his cheekbones very prominent. When you looked at him, you almost got the impression of weakness, but actually, he was very tough. The kind of person who could, and had, endured a lot of hard living. Narses took them straight to Orran.

Valdar had always thought it an honour to appear before the King but when he dragged open the doors of the Great Hall his honour and pride became subjected to horror. Valdar's horror was almost immediately replaced with compassion, as the King he served appeared so white, weak and older than his years. Valdar had not seen Orran or been to Tanath for nearly a year, and the marked contrast he saw in his sovereign disturbed him.

'Your majesty,' Valdar exclaimed, as he strode towards the King's throne, kneeling before him and kissing his hand.

Narses walked over to the window, he was always watching, having learnt under Dante.

'Valdar my trusty servant,' Orran began, raising his hands to greet him. 'I was afraid this would happen,' he continued, observing the expression on Valdar's face. 'The people here see me everyday, and the change I feel in my body has largely gone unnoticed ... well ... until recently. People now, however, believe I am sick because of the war we are facing. The truth is, I have been ill for some time, but now of all times it decides to rear its ugly head!'

Orran looked over to Ninian and back to Valdar and Botherick; his eyes were dark.

'I'm dying,' he said bluntly with a frail voice.

Botherick's head sunk, not knowing what to say or do, but Valdar glanced in desperation to Ninian. Ninian remained silent; the look on his face confirmed to Valdar all he did not want to hear.

'Who else knows of this matter?'

'Valdar,' Orran replied, 'you are to tell no one – not even Eramia knows the extent of these things, and I will not have her hear about it through ...' He cut himself short, shaking his head.

'Forgive me lord, but she will have to know the extent of your illness at some point, even if it's at your ...' he looked around uneasily '... your death. Not even the best men can hide that.'

Orran sat on his throne mumbling something to himself, with an expression on his face of understanding, one that comes from knowing more of a greater plan already thought through.

'Aaaah,' Orran suddenly begun, again raising his voice and motioning with his hand, 'It all depends on the manner of the death I receive.'

Botherick and Valdar did not understand at first, until Ninian offered them a little help. In his old familiar voice, Ninian looked upon the two men of war with pity and quietly said, 'Have you seen the ships that are off our coast? Their number? Their size? They have not come simply to pilfer our gold.'

'You think you may die in the struggle anyway?' inquired Valdar, first starring at the king then looking for Ninian's approval.

Ninian gestured with his hand, rolling it in front of him, prompting Valdar to go further.

'You plan to die … You *seek* a death in battle … to end your days with the brave.'

Although he said it rather sadly, he longed for the same himself when the time came and he even envied Orran, that his death would take place for so worthy a reason. Both Valdar and Botherick reflected on this plan.

Ninian interrupted their dreams of death by asking if they had seen Dante on the way to the castle.

'Not a days ride from here,' said Botherick.

'Who was with him?' asked Valdar. 'And why of all people is Dante leaving?'

Orran replied with a heaviness of heart.

'I sent Eramia and her maid away from the castle, for I fear this whole affair will be messy; not the place for a future queen, she need not experience such bloody carnage to reign well.'

'But why Dante?' Valdar asked again.

'How else could I lead the army from the front? If Dante were here, the men would want him in my place, and there was too great a risk he could actually protect me! If it's any comfort, he left under intense protestation and with much convincing from Ninian. But I doubt he would have left at all if he had known the full extent of my plans.'

'Aye,' said Botherick and Valdar simultaneously.

'He wasn't the happiest we had ever seen him,' added Botherick, with his eyebrows raised.

'Of that, I am sure,' said Orran, who came near to laughing.

Then, as with many times of impending danger, or of severe loss, like at funerals, there was a peculiar level of joy in the King's court. There was a reminiscing of people, times and places in the recent history of Greenhaven. Although, in a healthy way, a way that failed to exclude all hope.

With two simple questions however, Valdar managed to turn the whole conversation back to the matter at hand.

'You say you have seen the ships Ninian? Tell us everything you know.'

'There can be no doubt as to who they are; the serpent's heads on the front of their ships reveal their identity. It is what they are doing that concerns us most,' Ninian said, with a furrowed brow.

Valdar and Botherick gave Ninian their full attention; Orran sat on his throne with his hand across his forehead, focusing into nothing.

'They appear to be waiting,' Ninian continued.

'Hmmm,' Valdar responded, 'the Men of the North,' he said again as if speaking to himself but out loud. 'Their greatest weapon has been rumoured to be speed and surprise. Why are they waiting?'

'Reinforcements, getting ready, preparation, who cares?' said Botherick, 'It is giving us time to make Tanath practically impenetrable.'

'No, there must be something,' Valdar said, deep in thought.

'I agree,' Ninian was quick to add, before a moments silence descended in the Great Hall.

Orran stood up, drawing the other's attention to him.

'What they are doing, or what they are planning is not our primary concern. What we have to decide is what action we are going to take now. How many men have you brought with you from the eastern front?' he asked Valdar.

'About four hundred, my lord.'

'But the eastern border is well protected?'

'I left only eighty men,' he said, looking at Botherick as if to say that was ample. 'We haven't seen trouble for over ten months, and besides, those savages are in no condition to launch an attack, not after their defeat by our brothers from Reelig.'

Orran appeared slightly uneasy but trusted Valdar's judgment.

'What of the islands at the end of the bay?' the king questioned.

'I sent twenty men this morning,' said Narses, 'they should be ready by nightfall. They have enough arrows to cause considerable damage if the conditions are dry and the wind shows them favour.'

'Good … good,' said Orran, clasping his hands.

Narses bowed his head reverently; he was not one for words, even in times of turmoil.

'What numbers are we dealing with, does anyone know?' asked Valdar.

'There are nine battleships off the west of the islands as we speak but by their size, Narses reckons each one could hold a hundred men.' Ninian responded.

'A hundred men, are you sure?' said Botherick, in a tone of shocked disbelief.

Narses silently confirmed his estimation by slowly shutting his eyes and moving his head a fraction forward.

'More than double our number perhaps?' Valdar said, rhetorically.

'But the castle is in full state of defence?' asked Orran.

'The only thing we are waiting for is the attack to start,' muttered Narses.

'Does anyone know how it will begin?'

'Surely they will have to sail in, my lord,' Botherick answered, 'which makes me wonder whether we should have more men on the islands.'

'Is twenty enough?' said Valdar, sharing Botherick's concerns.

'As soon as one ship lands on the island, a hundred fighting men will secure the passage for the other ships. If those men on the islands manage to damage even a couple of ships before they run for their lives, so be it. They wont have time to retreat back here to the castle before the other ships are at out gates, and we need all the men we can muster here,' Narses explained. 'Are your men ready?' He continued.

'They prepare for war as we speak,' stated Valdar.

'At the next low tide, bring them across,' ordered Orran. 'That gives them until midnight to prepare. Can you manage that?' he asked.

'We had planned to bring them over in the morning, they are tired from traveling but we will aim for midnight if you desire.'

'The waiting will tire them more than the battle if it continues any longer,' Orran sighed. 'Go and get some rest for yourselves, who knows when you will sleep again? Then let us put an end to these warmongering hoards, that Greenhaven and the Distant Isles may once more live out its time in peace.'

'Can I see the defenses?' Valdar asked Narses, who stretched out his arm towards the door.

'Please,' he said.

Botherick, Valdar and Narses, toured the castle's walls, discussing tactics and strategies. Ninian retired to his room by the small chapel and sought strength from the Lord as he knelt down to pray. Orran made his way to the front of Tanath, his home, and looked across the short stretch of water to the wide golden beach and the woods beyond; tent after tent, activity, men, and the business of war painted the scene in front of him.

What will be left? He asked himself. *I am leaving Greenhaven at a time of such change … perhaps my inclusion is all part of it? I wonder what will become of it all. Tanath? Greenhaven? … Eramia? What will they say of me when I am gone? What will history say of me?'* Then he thought, *'History is not really fair, I have had such little time to make such huge decisions and yet I will be judged by history and history has all the time in the world!* Then he laughed to himself.

The beach below him bristled with activity.

Will we ever get the chance to look back and ask "why"? Will we want to in Glory? When even the experiences of this life have finally been revealed as purifying fires at worst and loving teachers at best. Will we even want to? Asked Orran.

With many other questions and thoughts, he stood there looking into the east, the pale blue sky of the end of the day introducing the first stars of the setting sun's work. He stood for a while, taking time just to look.

As the men lit fires on the beach before the castle, Orran suddenly felt cold and turned to go inside.

A time for war, and a time for peace, and also a time to eat, he joked with himself, and he disappeared down the spiral staircase, the dim light swallowing his shadow and the stone walls embracing the noise of his heavy steps. He went in, and it was night.

10
The Ghindred Unveiled

As Eramia, Sebastian and Hannah stood staring at the Ghindred, Dante moved forward to greet them.

'The Silent Shadow. Is not that what the legends have called you?' he asked.

'It depends on what people you ask,' was the reply, 'I think the terms thieves or murderers are the most common options.'

Eramia and Hannah felt ashamed, for they both had thought these things about the Ghindred. Although they felt uneasy, they could not draw their eyes away from them. The man's voice appeared strangely familiar to Eramia but he hid his face from her, still, she pondered these things in her heart. Hannah and Eramia expected to see savage-like clothes on the Ghindred, but these were different. The faces they could see were well weathered – men who had lived their whole lives outside under the mercy of the elements but their clothes were all of a similar fashion. They were of a dark green colour, with what looked like skilled tailoring of lighter leaves embroidered on their upper bodies. Eramia strained in the dark to get a better view, the leaves looked to her like ivy. A few of the men wore some kind of headdress, which left only their eyes visible; they appeared the most threatening to behold.

Dante continued talking to the man in front of him. Hannah, trying to listen to his conversation, only managed to hear the last few words.

'I fear time may already be pitched against us, plans are in motion, what must be done do quickly,' said the stranger from the Silent Shadow.

'We need to move,' Dante said, turning to Sebastian.

'Can you manage?' Sebastian asked Eramia.

Eramia nodded but her face revealed that she found the journey hard going. The Ghindred picked up Eramia's and Hannah's things, while others put the fire out and hide all traces of their being there. Sebastian stayed close to Eramia, as did Hannah.

'What about the horses?' asked Hannah, 'are we just to leave them alone?'

'Set them loose,' said Dante, 'Fhad will lead them back to Tanath. It's not the first time we have been separated only to find him waiting for me back at the castle!'

'There will be time for introductions and formal welcomes later, for now all you need to know is my name,' said the man of the Ghindred who earlier spoke with Dante. 'I am Torridon.'

As soon as he said his name, he moved off into the woods, Dante motioned with his hand for the other three to follow.

'As quickly and quietly as you can,' Dante whispered, as they drew close to him. The rest of the Ghindred followed close behind.

They moved at a steady pace through the woods all night, from tree to tree, rock to rock, and clearing to clearing. Not many hours had passed before Sebastian wondered how far they had travelled, while Eramia and Hannah wondered how far was left.

A slight change of hue in the sky's expanse revealed a beckoning dawn, and Torridon questioned to himself if they should not stop now for some rest. For at first and last light they were the most susceptible to attack from anyone who may have been tracing their footsteps. With the coming of dawn, there also came an intruding mist, which hung in the trees, taking away all sharp edges and making everything softer and vastly paler in appearance. It was refreshing to walk through but for some reason, it made the absence of noise all the more noticeable. Torridon pressed on.

They journeyed until the rising sun provoked the birds to song and the mist to flee, at which point Torridon watched for a place to rest. Hannah in particular, was ready to drop down and rest whenever Torridon could find it. Dante looked around him, the sky above was clear and of a rich blue colour, and could be made out only in between the myriad of branches competing for its space. The trees in this part of the wood were exceedingly old and thick moss like a velvet carpet clung to the floor. They were actually in the bottom of a large shallow depression, which was just low enough to take them out of vision of the surrounding area.

'Perfect,' said Torridon, 'we shall stop for a short rest here.'

'What news? Dante asked him.

'Not now Dante, you need to rest, you will meet with the elders shortly.'

Seeing Hannah and Eramia already asleep on the moss, Dante also settled down and shut his eyes. Sebastian watched from a short distance and was amazed that Dante went to sleep so quickly. Although the Ghindred were strangers to Sebastian, it was clear that Dante knew them well enough to rest easy and it was not long before Sebastian had joined the other three, trusting Dante's judgment regarding their scouts.

Torridon and the Silent Shadow gathered food and water for the remainder of the journey. Torridon then sent Lindfarll on ahead to the council of the elders at the meeting rock of Glamondon, or the Dancing Voices, as it was also known.

Eramia was the first to stir but she kept very still, thinking about everything that had happened over the last week. She thought she had life all sorted out, she thought she knew about the Ghindred, but she never thought she would be in love. Her world had changed. She now longed for some things of that old life, especially as she was cold and tired. Although her life was in many ways now harder, she felt she was no longer a child, and the realization of an unknown future actually gave her hope.

Eramia sat up and looked at Sebastian who lay sleeping at her feet. He looked so at peace, asleep on the moss, his hair fallen across his eyes. The wound to the back of his head, although quite clearly visible, detracted nothing from his youthful rugged beauty. Eramia wondered what future, if any, would be theirs to enjoy, or to endure, and she took Sebastian's hand in hers and kissed it, causing him to stir and smile, but not fully awake from his slumber.

A sudden movement through the trees caught Eramia's eye and she looked intently towards where the branches of the trees still shook. However, before she had a chance to see what caused the leaves to shake, she could hear Torridon's voice behind her.

'Your majesty,' he said, looking at her as she stared into the woods. 'Your majesty, we really must be moving again, would you care for some water or food?'

However, before Eramia had a chance to reply, Hannah who had not actually been asleep for some time, but who was still lying down, said, 'I'll attend to Lady Eramia. I'm still her maid even out of the castle.'

Torridon looked at her kindly.

'A young woman with a sense of duty and loyalty, very rare these days,' he said, smiling and a little surprised, 'hmmm … very rare indeed, you still serve your mistress well … very commendable.'

'She is more of a sister to me than a maid,' Eramia added, not wanting to appear spoilt or helpless.

'So I have noticed,' said Torridon, 'since you have entered the woods she has not failed to leave your side.'

'You have been watching us since the beginning?' asked Eramia.

Torridon then leaned over close to Eramia, out of earshot of Hannah.

'We have been watching you all your life,' he whispered in a low voice in Eramia's ear, looking around him for uninvited listeners.

Eramia sat back with an inquisitive expression on her beautiful face. She looked at the man in front of her, who still covered the majority of his face. Eramia shot a glance at Hannah who immediately dismissed herself from her mistress' presence, and turning back to Torridon Eramia tilted her head to one side, and gave him a look as if to say, *Go on.*

'Eramia,' he began, before falling into her deep brown eyes.

Eramia stared in astonishment as a tear formed in Torridon's eye and fell into his scarf.

'Eramia … it's been a long time since I last saw you and now many things must be revealed,' he said, removing the material from around his head.

His full head of silver hair was in marked contrast with the rich greens of the woods, and then his face was unveiled. Eramia's eyes widened, she stood up and drew back a little, trying to catch her breath at Torridon's revelation of his identity. Eramia raised her hand to her mouth.

'You,' she murmured, '… but you're … you're dead! … Is it really you? … *Lord* Torridon?' Then she remembered how from the start she had sensed a familiarity in his voice.

'I did not die, my Lady,' he said softly. 'I joined the Silent Shadow and have lived ever since to serve your father, and now you, as my calling has led me, and there are many things you must be told but I ask first of all that you accept my service and do not think me cruel to have let you believe I was dead.'

Then Torridon bent down on his knees and bowed at her feet.

Eramia leant down, and although still in shock, she lifted his face with her hand.

'How could I not be pleased? … For years I have wished you were still alive.'

Eramia and Torridon shared a deep joy that day; Hannah watched from behind a tree and Dante witnessed everything.

'Would you mind if I filled in some of the blanks along the way?' Asked Torridon, 'We really ought to be moving, we have been in the one place rather a long time.'

Dante appeared from nowhere and caught Eramia's eye as he stooped to wake up Sebastian. It was not a look that pleased Eramia, rather, the kind of belittling look an adult gives a child, when the child realizes something has been known by the parent for years.

'Sebastian ... its time,' and almost without waking up, Sebastian rose to his feet and instinctively searched round him for Eramia, who stood next to Torridon. Torridon gave a short whistle, much like the sound of a bird, and the remaining Ghindred made themselves visible, like creatures nobody sees until they move.

As they began to move, Sebastian went to join Eramia, but Dante grabbed him firmly back by the arm.

'Let her be Sebastian,' he advised, ' she needs to hear what Torridon has to say, things are not always as they seem and time can raise as many questions as it can heal wounds.'

Sebastian looked at Dante utterly confused. *Does he always have to be so cryptic, can't he dispense with the riddles, just once*, he thought.

Dante added plainly, 'Torridon is an old acquaintance and Eramia hasn't seen him in many years.'

As they walked, Sebastian kept his eye on this Torridon, watching as he and Eramia talked continuously.

'Do you know who he is?' Sebastian asked Hannah, who walked beside him.

'His face is familiar, I'm sure I have seen him at the Castle but I'm going back a good few years and could quite easily be mistaken,' Hannah replied.

The two walked on, side by side, in silence for some time.

'I hate not knowing things,' Sebastian blurted out all of a sudden.

Hannah smiled to herself.

'I think perhaps jealousy, not ignorance, may be the source of your anger.'

Sebastian looked at her, Hannah had stripped away all pretence and acting in a single sentence, and Sebastian knew in his heart that she was right.

'It is clear you love her, but to me, it is also clear that she loves you.'

This affirmation greatly pleased Sebastian, coming from one so close to his beloved and it put is heart at rest considerably.

Sebastian's mind, however, remained full of questions. As the group continued their journey, they came to a place where the ground before them stopped, the trees thinned and the light grew stronger. They found themselves on a ridge, with a path that took them down to where the Hala Issla flowed with rapids. They could easily see it shimmering below them.

The whole landscape opened up before Eramia and her subjects, and the dense woodland they had been previously traveling through, now looked quite dreary behind them. The Hala Issla's banks were about twenty foot in width, and it weaved its way through the woods below them like a giant silver eel in a massive pond of algae. The sun was almost level with them in the sky and the sweeping hills of the wood's northern edge were just visible in the haze.

Neither Hannah nor Eramia had seen so much land from one viewpoint, and they stared in awe at the enormous region that had been exposed to their eyes. Sebastian also stopped to take in the view, his eye was drawn to the small waterfalls and the tiny streams that trickled through the woods they had previously passed through and now fell cascading to their new homes in the valley.

'I'll never tire of seeing such sights,' Torridon said to Eramia, 'but let's keep moving nonetheless.' And he placed his hand on her lower back, beckoning her to continue with him.

Sebastian saw this innocent gesture and was consumed with envy.

The few members of the Silent Shadow led Eramia, Sebastian and Hannah down the narrow and precarious path, and it was little more than that, to try to reach the council of the elders by last light. The three were all feeling tired now but Sebastian noted how Dante could just keep going on and on, with no complaining and no need for much rest. He began to wander how closely he was involved with the Ghindred and this Silent Shadow group, *whoever they were*, he thought, never having heard of them.

'I suppose you're wondering what became of me all those years ago?' Torridon asked Eramia, as the two walked alone, 'Twelve years has it been? Twelve years!' he repeated, almost shocking himself.

Eramia looked at him, not quite knowing what to say or what she was about to find out.

'I remember crying when they told me you had died … Does my father know you are still alive? No … no, he cannot know … he was very depressed for a while when he found out you were dead.'

'Aye … your father and I were very close. I am sorry for the pain I caused him … and you, you must know it has hurt me terribly, thinking of all the years I have missed watching you grow up.'

'You were like family to me …'

'And you to me, my Lady … and maybe we would all do things differently if we had the chance to go back? … I don't know. Believe me, it has not been easy swapping the luxuries of riches for the woods. Many times I have longed to be back in my old life … with old friends,' Torridon answered reflectively.

'Then why didn't you?' Eramia asked quite unsympathetically.

'Have you heard of the Silent Shadow?'

'Not in name, not before yesterday that is.'

'Not in name?' Torridon inquired.

'I heard conversations in the castle that, well, let's just say were not for my ears. There was talk of some secret society or group or gathering that worried my father, but I had always given it over to fairytales and legends. Besides, if it were true, Dante, Ninian or my father, would have found out between them, and they both reassured him there was nothing to worry about.'

'Your father is wiser than you think, my Lady, and here is a lesson on how to rule well when you are queen, always keep watching, always listen. Your father was right to suspect that we existed, he was wrong to take Ninian and Dante's words on board so readily.'

Eramia turned to Torridon with wide opened eyes,

'Are you saying *they* have betrayed my father?'

'No … no Eramia, would they, would I, betray your father? Seventeen years I served him – could he find fault with me in that time?'

Torridon was disturbed even by Eramia's suggestion, 'We serve the King of Greenhaven …' he forthrightly stated.

'We?' interrupted Eramia, 'I don't understand?'

'The Silent Shadow.'

'That I understand, I meant who are the "we",' and she turned to look at Dante who was gathering pace behind them.

Torridon looked upon Eramia as if she was the child he once remembered her being,

'Dante doesn't know *about* us,' he said, shaking his head, 'O no, much more than that.'

Eramia stopped.

'He's one of us.'

The rest of the party caught up and gathered around Eramia. This time, as Eramia turned to look at Dante, she found him standing right behind her, and anger came over her like a gathering storm.

'You pretend to serve my father, what, with lies and deceit, hiding things from him? How could you! He trusted you Dante, he trusted you with everything ... even me!'

Eramia's voice had risen in her anger and she beat Dante's chest with her fists as tears rolled down her cheeks.

'How could you?' she sobbed.

'No, my Lady, you don't understand,' Torridon was quick to add, 'He does, we do, the Silent Shadow that is, its purpose is to serve the King of Greenhaven, in this case your father.'

Dante placed his hands on Eramia's shoulders.

'Look at me,' he said, and Eramia couldn't for hate. 'Look at me.'

Eramia raised her tear-filled eyes, her teeth grinding.

'The Silent Shadow has to be this way, if the King, and it wont always be your father, Eramia, if the King knew about us he could control us and our power to help guide him would be lost. Eramia, your father could practically live without our aid. In many ways, he has made us redundant these last few decades. He is a good King, of noble blood. Nevertheless, Kings before him, and after, may be wicked and cruel men, and then our power is needed most, for the sake and peace of Greenhaven. I know this must all come as a shock to you, people you thought were dead are alive, and your father's closest friends in a secret society, and ...'

'Friends,' said Eramia interrupting, 'who else is involved?'

Torridon looked at Dante as he held Eramia's stare.

'Ninian,' Dante added, 'he too is of the Silent Shadow.'

Sebastian nearly chocked. Eramia wept. Sebastian, looking at Eramia, stepped up beside her.

'It's all too much for her Dante, can't you see?' he said, raising his voice.

At which point Eramia turned to Sebastian, and taking a few paces back, raised her hands in the air and sighed deeply, but Sebastian looked at her puzzled.

'You also?' she barely voiced.

'No! Dante and Sebastian said in unison.

'I'd not heard of them before yesterday,' exclaimed Sebastian, walking towards her, 'honest.'

Although he need not have added the word honest, as Eramia could see he meant what he said, and besides, she really did trust him. With this, Eramia threw her arms around Sebastian, trying not to cry any more, trying to be strong. Sebastian held her close to his body and kissed her forehead.

'Everything has changed forever,' she whispered into his chest, sobbing.

'Not everything,' Sebastian whispered back, 'I still love you.'

Eramia held him tightly, as Hannah, Dante and the others stood by awkwardly watching.

'Come on,' Sebastian said, reassuring her, 'we will go on together.'

Hannah drew alongside her mistress and the three set off following Torridon again. Nature witnessed this young woman's distress when a stag, hearing their commotion, stopped to stare in their direction. Torridon had already moved away, walking on ahead with his shoulders hunched, not wanting to see Eramia so hurt. Eramia felt faint.

11

The King's Armour

The clouds gathered in from the west, as Orran, Ninian and Narses watched the troops preparing to cross from the beach to the castle. The clanging of metal, the flickering and movement of torches, the low-level grumble of a multitude of voices;

'The sound of war,' Orran said to Ninian, 'Who knows what now awaits us?'

'What does it really matter?' replied Ninian. 'The events and circumstances of this life are rarely under our control, as long as we do that which is good and act with courage, what more are we called to?'

Orran's mind would have lingered on these words were it not for the fact of Botherick's bellowing voice from the base of the Castle, swallowing up any remaining silence of the night.

'First section, ready to cross, on my orders, march!'

The camp guards on the rear of the beach, when they saw the first troops cross to the castle, started banging their drums. Boom, ta ta ta boom, boom. Boom, ta ta ta boom, boom.

Orran looked grim faced as he watched the random torch lights fall into file and head towards the castle's causeway. Narses placed his hand on Ninian's shoulder, which caused the old man to turn, but without saying a word, Narses left the wall and went to position the army with Valdar and Botherick.

Botherick's voice could still occasionally be heard shouting orders to the remaining men on the mainland. The beat of the drums faded only when the last man had crossed to reach Tanath's mighty fortifications. The castle had turned from a home to a fortress almost over night. Archers lined the southern and northern walls, and each was busy gathering and positioning their arrows and defences. The western defences based themselves primarily in the garden Eramia so loved. Fighting troops, ready to attack any enemy storm of the castle, now filled the garden; three massive boulder throwing catapults capable of snapping a ship's mast in half, now stood dominant where the cherry blossom trees once flourished in all their solitary beauty.

When Narses was satisfied with the way Valdar and Botherick prepared their men, he left them to it, and went to find Orran. The King was standing in the walled garden talking to the knights of Greenhaven.

'My lord Orran,' Narses called, interrupting the King's conversation with the army.

'One moment Narses,' he said, raising his arm without turning round, 'I am speaking with the knights of Greenhaven!'

With these few wisely chosen words Orran lifted the men's spirits, filling them with pride and valour, not for what they may do but for what they were now, at that moment, at that time of all times.

As monarchs went, Orran was widely appreciated. This was not because he increased Greenhaven's borders, nor brought the kingdom much wealth, but because he maintained its historic reputation and sought to instill dignity and moral uprightness in every subject of the land. The people could see he believed in Greenhaven and them as its people.

After Orran had continued a few minutes with the men, he then turned to Narses, who stood alone on the lawn of the walled garden – half his figure illuminated by the influx of torches placed and carried about Tanath and half concealed in the night's darkness. Orran could not help thinking that here before him stood a man who was ready to die; he was a ferocious warrior who would not leave the battlefield until the end, either way. He was in charge of defending the southern hill-land before being brought to the castle and had gained a reputation for completing his business at whatever cost. He forced the warring clans who dwelt in the hills to make peace with each other on pain of death, and many of them had died by Narses' hand as he strived to maintain law. The law of averages would have had him as a dead man ten times over by now.

Who knows? Orran said to himself, *to what extent this will be the last battle?*

Orran walked towards Narses. Narses rattled his sheathed sword against his armour.

'*Your* armour is waiting for you in the Great Hall, my lord.'

'Ah yes,' said Orran, 'Time to put on some weight!'

'But what a weight of glory, my lord,' Narses was quick to affirm.

The two men walked through the castle's empty corridors, quite knowing neither what to say nor how to feel. Both had thought the King's decision to die in battle courageous and honourable, they just hadn't really considered all the details – Orran was getting dressed for the last time, he was putting on the clothes in which he *would* die.

Orran began to wonder if he would be able to bear his armour, for he knew in his body his strength was fast leaving him and he was getting increasingly breathless. Narses noticed the heaviness of Orran's breath by the time they had reached the doors of the Great Hall. The absence of speech was accentuated with each intake and exhaling of breath, like death itself was echoing through Tanath's cool stone walls.

As Narses pushed open the heavy doors with considerable effort, they were met by Ninian who came walking towards them.

'It is ready,' he said, and as he moved to one side, Orran entered the Great Hall; there in front of him it stood, shining silver armour, resplendent in every way.

His white over-garment was attached to the mail, emblazoned with the green shield with *Seasaidh Sinn Ar Tir* written in white across it, next to that stood his sword, shield and helmet.

'Such beautiful clothes for such ghastly work,' murmured Orran, as he walked over and picked up his sword and drew it from its sheath. Where once the sword in his hand would have given him power and delight, it now only revealed the extent of his ever-increasing weakness and the ephemeral nature of life. He placed it back in its sheath and rested it on the floor.

'My sword I will take ... my helmet and shield can wait for me in my tomb,' he said dryly, 'for all the use it will be then.'

'Ah,' Ninian began, 'even if you could take it with you, it would be swallowed up by the glory of another and appear to you as rusted tin and corroded iron. And there is no shame in longing for that hope.'

'What you say I know is true my dear friend,' Orran said kindly, 'but one thing I have found to be quite strange and unexpected.'

Ninian faced him with interest.

'When it came to dying, I always thought I would think on nothing but heaven, yet, it's the matters of earthly business that fill my concerns – the here and now, the daily necessities of this life.'

'And that seems strange to you?' asked Ninian, in a way which made Orran think it probably shouldn't have worried him.

'Heaven is a coming home, not a going away, it's the place where the things which made you *you* now, are made *you* in a fuller more glorious sense, the *you* God always wanted you to be … perhaps even now. This is the mist at dawn, the pale blue of twilight, the smoking embers of the night before – then … Oh, then, then will be the rising sun, the brightest of days, and the everlasting flame! … But it starts here, dear friend, not as in the beginning of a story so much as in the prologue.'

Ninian, with his hands clenched and looking upwards, let his eyes fill freely with tears, being lost in the glory of his vision.

'I never did set enough time aside just to think,' Orran said, quite jealous of his friend's well mastered art.

As Orran looked like he too was about to set off on some grand mental journey, Narses, the most silent friend a man could ever have and still enjoy, chose this moment to exercise his deep voice and concern.

'This time, my lord, the time to think has perhaps been overshadowed by the time to act?' Prompting the King to adorn his armour, or as much as he could carry.

Orran nodded heavily. Slowly removing his outer garments, he made way for the new but he was slow and awkward in his actions. Narses made his way across the hall to help him, and thought to himself, *I hope the battle starts soon,* for Orran's sake.

Ninian watched uncomfortably until his heart unexpectedly broke down inside, of which Orran seemed to be aware. For Ninian, it was like watching an old lion being ousted from the pride; there was still size, nobility and proven character present, but the strength was fading fast, in turn touching slightly on dignity.

'When the time comes, call me. I will be in the chapel tonight,' Ninian said, quickly leaving Narses to deal with any final adjustments of the King's armour, and he headed for the door, knowing it was his duty to stay.

Don't leave me now, Orran thought in desperation, but as Ninian's back disappeared out of the doorway, he could not quite bring himself to call out his name, and he did not want to burden his friend anymore.

Seeing the King's face however, played on Narses' sense of responsibility and without thinking, he said,

'Shall *I* stay, my lord?'

Orran opened his mouth but stopped short of saying a word.

Certain situations need certain friends for certain reasons, he thought, *I could cope with Dante being here, and where is Eramia? … Ninian, come back!*

Narses waited for an answer.

'I think … I think I should rest,' he affirmed to himself. 'Besides, I need you to make sure Valdar and Botherick have all they need for the defence of Tanath. Give them whatever they need, I'd rather they had it all than those northern barbarians, brute beasts, war mongers …' He said, his face twisted with wrinkles, wrought with frowns.

'As you will,' replied Narses, who left the king in the Great Hall, alone on the throne of the great royals of Greenhaven, a seat of history, the bearer of kings.

12

The Gathering of the Silent Shadow

Eramia hardly said a word and no one asked her any questions. Sebastian stayed as close to her as possible, as did Hannah. Torridon could feel the tension, and it became a burden to him, like an oak log straddled across his shoulders but he could not bring himself to speak. Dante followed a few paces behind, little fazed him and to be honest, he quite welcomed the silence. He could physically see Torridon's discomfort with the whole situation and his longing for words to make amends.

That's the diplomat in him, Dante thought to himself, *it has never left him.*

Indeed, Torridon had been one of Orran's closest allies as a member of the King's council, soothing away many a border dispute with words rather than war.

The remaining members of the Silent Shadow that accompanied Torridon and the party led them down the mountain side into the thinner woods where the Hala Issla cut its route in the valleys below. The trees in some places on this side of the mountains grew more sparsely, many of them being young trees and saplings. These trees were still tall but the atmosphere was far less gloomy compared to some of the stretches of wood they had walked though. However, the ground was a lot boggier where the younger trees grew and a damp smell hung in the air and more insects than usual flew about their faces. The ground below them was much more uneven, clumps of turf covering the roots of older, fallen trees, adding further strain to their trek.

Eramia stopped and leant against a tree.

'We need to stop and rest,' Sebastian said immediately.

'It's not far,' Dante said walking past them, 'we're nearly there.'

'Just a few minutes,' said Hannah, herself feeling the struggle.

'What's five minutes?' Torridon chipped in, seeking to appease Eramia.

Dante walked through the whole group until he was at the front with the lead scout.

'A few minutes,' he said, reluctantly.

Everything seemed to happen so quickly the last couple of days Sebastian had trouble remembering how many days they had been traveling, where they were going, and at times, even for what reason. Hannah and Sebastian had spoken together along the way of what might await them at this council of elders, and this Glamondon. Sebastian was also looking forward to getting some answers. Hannah wondered if after everything, she would be left with only a lot more questions. Eramia did not say much on the subject but had worked out that Dante and Ninian from the start had planned all this, even though the end of their plan eluded her. All three harboured deep hopes and fears regarding the Silent Shadow.

Anything secretive immediately aroused suspicion in Eramia, however, Hannah loved the notion that a secret organization of warriors existed, dwelling in Greenhaven all her life. The entire state of affairs seemed for Hannah as if reality had jumped out of a favourite bedtime story – a well loved tale turning out to be history.

Sebastian prayed for wisdom in all things and prayed it often. The walking for all three appeared endless. Of course, as with any excursion, time passes a lot slower when you have no idea of how long you will be traveling. Dante, nevertheless, was right, it was not too much further to their destination's end and the meeting place of the council of the Silent Shadow. Before too long, Eramia, Hannah and Sebastian, arrived at their journey's objective.

The last part of their walk saw them move from the younger trees of thin trunks and wispy branches, back to a part where the trees had grown for centuries. However, they were not packed close together, as when they first entered the eastern woods, these grew in relative freedom from each other, not fighting for sunlight and rain, but each standing proud in the space it dominated. Giant oaks, elm, horse chestnut and pine trees, interspersed with flowers, shrubs and plants that carry berries. It was quite a colourful setting in spring. The sun beams fell through the widely spread branches onto the tall grass which covered the floor. The many little buzzes of hard working flies and insects dimly played their continuous tunes. An intermittent breeze cooled their faces from the tiring walk, taking with it the flies that hung about their heads.

The trees all around them, those ancient fellows of the wood, suddenly gave way, flooding the area before them in what seemed like excessive light. They all screwed up their faces, narrowing their eyes, even though they were desperate to keep them open. The trees gave way to grass, which in turn gave way to rock, and it looked to Eramia as if the area had been tiled, for the rock was so smooth and flat, an expanse of glistening granite like the sun shining on snow.

The rock itself was about twenty eight foot wide at its furthest reach, but in contrast to the forest they had walked through it felt incredibly spacious. In fact, to Sebastian, it felt dangerously open. If it wasn't for Torridon leading them straight to it, Sebastian would have steered well clear. There were men already on the rock, and those present turned to see their expected guests, their heads turning one by one. Those of the Silent Shadow who had been traveling with Eramia, Hannah and Sebastian, went straight over to join their fraternity with obvious familiarity. Dante went over to an old man who stood with the support of two others at the edge of the trees in the shade.

Hannah looked at the forty or so men with the eyes of a child on Christmas morning. Apart from the tiredness, she loved the adventure. Eramia could not quite decipher how she felt, yet almost unconsciously she reached out for Sebastian's hand and held it tight, but hidden behind his back.

'Stay close to me,' she whispered to him.

Sebastian's heart was both warmed and refreshed by her need of him. The three lingered where they stood, all eyes were upon them as silence fell on the remote gathering. Eramia felt angry with herself for not being as forceful a presence as she had always likened herself to be, yet she still managed to muster the words,

'I am Eramia, the heir of Greenhaven, daughter of King Orran. Who are you? And what do you want?'

The old man Dante had greeted then struggled to his feet and tried to take a few steps forward.

'We are what have become known as the Silent Shadow. Please, step forward.'

Eramia was astonished that a person who looked so physically frail still maintained such a strong voice.

'Please,' he said again, beckoning them with his skeletal hand.

Eramia's hand slipped out of Sebastian's grip as she hesitantly took a few paces forward. As she took those steps, the old man continued to speak.

'We are the Silent Shadow, servants of Greenhaven … your servants your majesty,' as he bowed his head low.

All the others also bowed, down on their knees with their faces to the ground. Eramia was a little taken back by this – even Dante was found at her feet. On seeing the Silent Shadow bowing so low, Sebastian and Hannah felt compelled to join them but mainly out of shocked embarrassment.

'We exist for your service and your good, my Lady, from us you have nothing to fear. However … there are others in these parts and no one would think less of you for fearing them, and they are set on your destruction, which is why you are here.'

'And you?' Eramia addressed the Silent Shadow, 'Why are you here? Why serve my father in secret? She asked.

'Greenhaven has its own warriors, its own army,' Hannah unexpectedly added.

Eramia raised her hand only a little but it was enough for Hannah to know not to speak again.

'Warriors?' The old man repeated with a smile on his face; a kind face in Eramia's opinion, not unlike Ninian's. 'Warriors!' he said again, awkwardly raising both his feeble arms. 'We are not all like Dante or Torridon here; I could barely lift a sword let alone wield one! No, no, no. My name is Comasius my dear, I, with the other elders lead these men standing before you; our task, our objective, is to make Greenhaven a safe and prosperous place to live, a place where honest men can live without fear and tyranny, in a land which knows justice and is willing for it to be exercised. Why you may ask yourself? Because we love this land that God has entrusted to us to live in.'

'You fear God?' Eramia said, with her eyebrows raised.

Comasius looked at her, his eyes as old as they were still managed to pierce her soul, and she quickly said the first thing that sprang into her mind.

'You want a heaven on earth?'

'Oh no,' said Comasius, shaking his head, 'heaven will always be heaven and not earth, even if for some people it begins here, but you are a very perceptive young lady for one so young, and in part you are right. Many of us would love to see Greenhaven exhibiting the character of the kingdom of heaven but not all of us are Christians. There are those among us who act out of a patriotic duty, men like Dante here, a man of war in a desire for peace, or Shamgar there, a lover of justice.' He said, pointing with his bony finger, the skin stretched tight and almost translucent.

Eramia interrupted Comasius, mustering all the eloquence and dignity she could, saying quite sternly,

'Tell me; is justice, peace and the kingdom of God likely to be found among those who deceive their King?' And glancing at Dante, she added, 'Their friend?'

'We are friends who meet for a common cause, where is our deception? We do no wrong.'

'Groups of friends do not usually posses names, especially one so sinister.'

'The Silent Shadow was a name put upon us, it's more of a description … or a fear … given to us by those who dwell outside the wood. Just like the Ghindred, those who mistake us and the things we do, being ignorant of our intentions, demonize us. But I admit, it is an appropriate name, we shadow the King of Greenhaven in silence, seeking to influence his rule.'

'A group of friends with elders?' said Eramia, both hands on her hips and in a tone of increasing agitation.

'No more than a description of us elderly ones who are shown respect due to our age,' said Comasius, trying to put Eramia at ease, but continued, 'Well, that's how it all started back in the days of Greenhaven's beginnings, many centuries ago.'

'Go on,' Eramia said, practically demanding.

'Through reputation, traditions and time, we have become what we are now, but it did all start with a few friends who saw the potential Greenhaven had in its early years, to become either a great kingdom or a depraved kingdom. After the noble kings died and the house of Lewis fell, for four generations wicked men did sit upon the throne that now belongs to your father. Four generations of the sons of Cain nearly ruined this country. If it wasn't for the founders of our present gathering, who knows what would have happened. When the fourth heir of Cain's seed came to the throne, he was set on expansion and war, but Malcom, his advisor, along with other prominent men who knew the wickedness of the King's heart and had witnessed the years of oppression under his fathers, hatched a plot with Luther of Dreams to overthrow the King.'

'Then it was treason, and you den of thieves and murderers are condemned by your own history,' said Eramia.

'Their actions saved the lives of hundreds of innocent men, women and children, and we have done so ever since, although never again did we remove a King or Queen by force,' said Comasius, desperately hoping he was correct. 'And since the Ghindred were established and enlisted to aid the king, we have simply worked as part of them; we are by ancient law, Ghindred.'

'I thought you honoured the King? With dethronement?' Eramia replied.

'Honour is earned. It can be lost, it can be taken away.'

Eramia shook her head.

'Try to understand,' pleaded Torridon, 'We work for that which is good …'

'Good for whom?'

'… and right, that which is beneficial to this land and to its people. As such, we love your father and serve him gladly. We have suffered many a foolish and unwise King, we never thought of removing them.'

'We shall serve you gladly,' Comasius said to Eramia.

Silence descended on the gathering as Eramia thought through all that had been said.

'Who was placed on the throne in exchange for the line of Cain?' She asked.

'That would have been Hector, who was the grandfather of Thoran; he made the official agreement with us to dwell in these woods. Thoran heard from Hector how their family had attained the throne of Greenhaven, when Hector lay dying, before Castle Tanath was even built.'

'When I am queen,' Eramia began, looking at Comasius, Torridon and Dante, then thinking of Ninian and desperately wanting to say, *you shall no longer exist,* 'when I am queen, perhaps things may change,' she said, lifting her head high.

'Why do you think I brought you here,' Dante asked Eramia in a tone touched with anger, surprising her. 'Not since Thoran has a Queen or King even known of our existence; why risk telling you? Why now?'

Eramia sought urgently for an answer but stood silent before everyone and Dante, who looked her straight in the eye.

'When you become queen indeed,' interrupted Comasius, whose voice had become that of an old man again, a grandpa with words of comfort. 'The time has come. No more waiting, no more preparation, now is the time my Lady to arise and be Queen. This will be the place of your coronation!'

Hannah shot a glance at Eramia who genuinely looked in a state of shock.

'Madness … Dante what is he talking about? Have you all gone mad?' Eramia said, looking around at them in disbelief, her hands on her head.

Hannah and Sebastian were looking at each other with utter amazement.

'What's going on?' Hannah mouthed to him, but he just stared at her shaking his head and shrugging his shoulders.

'My dear child,' said Comasius, 'You had better sit down.'

Those who stood nearby brought some furs for Eramia and the others to sit on; Comasius seated himself among the bluebells on a section of log cut from a large tree. Dante and Torridon joined Comasius and two other elders, as the rest of the Silent Shadow disappeared into the woods, out of sight, in earshot.

In the presence of the elders, Dante unveiled recent events, plans and movements. Some of the information he had only found out himself since he left Tanath, by a letter Ninian had passed to him in a book the last time Dante left the Great Hall. Eramia, Hannah and Sebastian sat speechless, as Dante, uncharacteristically gentle, revealed the truth of their present situation. How war with the Men of the North was immanent and had been suspected for some time, and how he and Ninian, with the guidance of the elders, had planned to bring Eramia to Glamondon to have her crowned as Queen on the inevitable death of her father. Dante also explained that the Men of the North were far too many for the soldiers of Greenhaven to attack. Their only hope was in defence, in Tanath's mighty walls. Even Dante could not tell Eramia about her father's illness without himself shedding a tear.

Sebastian was surprised to find out that Ninian sent him along with Eramia so there would be a man of God present for the coronation. Hannah was slightly angry with herself for not being aware of any of it, for she prided herself on knowing the affairs of the King's court, much to Ninian and Dante's disdain. Despite the overwhelming revelations Dante made, he also pressed the urgency of their present predicament and the necessity of making some difficult decisions that would fall to Eramia's discretion.

The small gathering at Glamondon could plainly see the burdens that Eramia was carrying. The youthful vigor of her usual vibrant countenance was now masked with a serious thoughtfulness quite appropriate for one so young at such a time as this, for one in such a position as hers.

'Will we give you a little space to rest and think things over?' suggested Comasius, 'But Dante is right, time may well be against us. We shall meet together again later this afternoon, by which time a plan *must* be in place … it must … and then carried out.'

His aging eyes surrounded by the army of wrinkles that occupied the expression on his face.

'My Lady, I may just add, there will be time to mourn for your father but now requires strength and courage from you.'

Eramia looked at the old man and was surprised that in her heart she trusted him.

'I will act,' she said, with an heir of authority, 'and you shall know my decision.'

After Eramia had said this, Dante and the elders got up and left. A grey cloud engulfed the sun and heaviness surrounded Eramia's heart. Hannah and Sebastian ran over to join her, each taking a hand, neither knowing quite what to say.

13
Sebastian Weeps

As Dante broke away from Comasius and the others, Sebastian made his way though the trees to talk with him. He passed by Eramia, placing his hand on her lower back, causing her to both smile and sigh, it felt to her like the touch and warmth of the sun after heavy rain.

'Come on,' Eramia said to Hannah, 'we have at last truly great things to discuss of our own.'

'I know,' replied Hannah, 'but I never realized that in all the great stories and accounts of old, the pain and struggles from which the greatness always arose were such a large and constant part of the story.'

'I think we are all too aware of how frightfully dull an easy life can be,' said Eramia, who remembered how many times the two of them desperately sought something to do at Tanath.

Then the two young women became engrossed in conversation, the recent events, their plans, and their future. However, their child-like familiarity of old had been unconsciously replaced with graveness suitable to the weight of their present situation.

Dante heard Sebastian before he even reached him, and he stopped without turning round, until Sebastian caught up.

'Tell me Dante, if I have earned your trust, tell me everything.'

Dante knew better than anyone that the fullest picture was always the most preferred and he found a connection with Sebastian in his willingness to know. Ever since his perception of the Ghindred fundamentally changed all those years ago, Dante always sought to know as much as he could about anything that crossed his path.

'Come. Walk with me,' Dante urged Sebastian, taking him by the elbow and leading him further away from his beloved Eramia. So the two men walked side by side, war and peace sharing knowledge, conversing.

'It all started a few years ago,' began Dante. 'Rumours … sightings out on the Distant Isles and by the Ghindred … a strange stirring in these woods.'

'The Men of the North?' asked Sebastian.

'Yes. We sighted the odd ship off the coast at first, but soon smaller vessels were sailing up the Hala Issla and scouting parties were exploring the land, even up to the towns! We did not know what to do at first, neither Orran nor the Silent Shadow, so we waited and watched. It was they who had been killing the deer and the cattle, even some of the Ghindred have been taken as slaves and been forced to lead them through the woods.'

'How have the Silent Shadow survived?'

'Well, thankfully, although they seem to be potentially great in number and armed to the teeth, they are also very loud and quite undisciplined. More than once, Torridon tells me, they have crept into their camp, right next to their boats and gathered information in the last few days.'

'And can you understand any of it? Has it been of any use?'

'Very little I'm afraid, no one we know can read their language, but Torridon, from his days in the King's court did manage to learn a little of their mother tongue.'

'How would that help though?'

'Think about it, what talks in their language?'

'Only them I suppose … Ah, you *took* some of *them*?' Sebastian said, guessing correctly.

'Exactly, I'm afraid they have lost the odd man over the last few days but our picture of events has been ever growing. From what we understand, the main part of their force is to attack Tanath by sea.'

'Kill the shepherd, scatter the sheep.'

'Quite. However, at the same time, they plan to send a few hundred men to march on Castle Tanath via the Hala Issla. Well, this is the latest Torridon told me yesterday.'

'But all our troops are at Tanath!' exclaimed Sebastian. 'The towns are defenceless!'

'No, said Dante, shaking his head, 'not all of them. Apart from the Silent Shadow, I have kept my regiment near the towns on the edge of the eastern woods; they are keeping supplies and horses for us.'

'Then what about us … the Silent Shadow I mean,' asked Sebastian.

'You were right the first time,' Dante grinned, 'we have my regiment's horses waiting for us on the road back to Tanath, as soon as the Men of the North start to move we will ride to the beach at Tanath Castle and wait to meet them in battle there.'

'When do you expect them to land in our country?'

Dante looked at him, almost shocked, realizing Sebastian had not grasped the urgency of their predicament.

'They have already landed,' he said, 'they are *here* now.'

Sebastian's eyes opened wide, his face made pale, almost grey.

'Then why are we still here?' he cried.

'They are on foot, unused to the land and will move slowly. Nevertheless, Tanath will soon be under attack, they have only been waiting until these men are in position. These are the worst men of all, the ones who go in near the end to clean up the situation, to remove all traces of whatever stood before. The attack starts from the sea and once it starts, the King *will* die in battle.'

'How can you be so sure? Sebastian asked, unsure of Dante's certainty.

'He is dying Sebastian. His weakness in recent months will not improve and he would rather die fighting than of an illness, on his feet and not in bed. He is a King, he has a glory.'

Sebastian thought back to Rastko, his bludgeoned body distorted with pain.

'I can't see that glory anymore,' said Sebastian quietly.

Dante looked at his newfound friend, his own mind rekindling a hundred people's last moments that he himself bore witness and took.

'It's a regrettable glory … but a glory nonetheless, and one I hope to share some day.'

The two men paused and looked at each other. Sebastian placed his hand on Dante's shoulder.

'No man's path is exactly the same,' said Sebastian, as they made their way back to the others.

Hannah listened to Eramia as she thought through what to do; her world had been shaken violently. Her voice was cold and her movements rigid. No words about her father's soon to be death passed her mouth, but Hannah knew her well enough to know that she was thinking about the King; she kept fiddling with the ring Orran had given her when she turned eighteen.

'Eramia,' said Hannah, interrupting Eramia's flow of self contained dialogue. 'It would not be considered a weakness to mourn for your father,' she said softly.

Eramia closed her lips, wetting them with her tongue as if her throat were parched, and bit her bottom lip ever so gently. A tear fell from her eye, melting away her steely glare and she looked so vulnerable to Hannah.

'I must be strong,' Eramia managed to croak.

'And in what would you measure strength? With indifference? By losing all emotions? Forsaking all that is natural in being human? Passion and emotion, strong feelings and vulnerability, it is these very things that make you so strong Eramia. Stronger than I could ever be … A heart that can feel pain is a healthy one,' she added.

'I always thought I could be queen and would be a strong ruler …'

'You will be! O you will be!' Hannah declared, grabbing both Eramia's hands. 'Remember you are not alone in this, we are all with you, and the whole of Greenhaven favours you! Just think of the admiration you receive at the summer fairs!'

Eramia wiped away the tears from her cheeks and tried her hardest to compose herself.

'For my father's sake I hope you are right,' she said quietly, almost to herself.

'We shall all soon know,' Hannah replied with a sweet smile on her pretty face, 'for tomorrow you shall be Queen.'

'Yes,' Eramia said, immediately in response. 'It is my duty … and I hope also my joy,' she thought. 'Yes, tomorrow I shall be Queen. Come what may …' she said, thinking of all that could happen in the not too distant future. 'I will be Queen, if but for a day.'

'No one would deny the immensity of the burden you carry, but you shall never carry it entirely alone. Do all that God would put in your heart to do, and do it well.'

'I shall reign as my father before me. To love justice and mercy and to walk humbly with my God,' said Eramia, thinking of Orran and all that Ninian had taught her.

While she said these things Hannah noted a determination in her voice, and once more, the monarch replaced the little girl.

'First, I must speak with Sebastian alone,' Eramia said.

For all of Hannah and Eramia's familiarity, their friendship and love, Hannah never lost her reverence for Eramia and she was never displeased to serve her mistress.

'It is your coronation tomorrow my Lady, we have many things we must organize.'

'Call Comasius, tell him I will be Queen!' Eramia said to Hannah, walking away.

Therefore, Hannah ran off to tell Comasius and the elders, among who stood Dante and Sebastian. Hannah explained all that she needed for preparing the ceremony and discussed times and a host of other matters suited to arranging a coronation for a queen.

Sebastian gave himself leave from the others and found Eramia under the bough of an aging elm tree.

'My Lady would be Queen?' he said slowly, not wishing to startle her. 'Then what will become of us?' he inquired.

'I must be Queen,' said Eramia, who loved the man that stood before her, 'and will not your vow ever keep us apart?' she said, in a cool emotionless tone, as if an unexpected frost had fallen on a spring dawn.

Sebastian knew she spoke the truth but the way she said it hurt him; it was like a foul medicine, required but hard to swallow. As he thought on her answer the two of them walked slowly round and round the tree, not side by side as both would have perhaps preferred, but on opposite sides of the trunk. Sebastian's hand trailed on the peeling bark and he hoped Eramia's hand would meet his there. He laughed to himself, if only in despair, as his hand moved round the body of the tree. It was as if that present scene was a parable of their future – both moving together, tantalizingly close, desperately wishing to touch and be close, if only for a moment, yet forever unable. Sebastian was sorely tempted to break his vow and forsake his vocation but even in his desperation, he knew in his heart Eramia would never let him, and he himself would never be truly fulfilled if he did – his thoughts confused him.

'You will be as close to me as Ninian is to my father,' said Eramia, *and in my heart, closer still*, she thought, but her outward appearance was stern, and where once a warm smile had greeted Sebastian, now stood a queen, and only a queen. Piercing eyes and tightly closed lips

— only the colour of Eramia's cheeks suggested any warmth. No lover found here, here was only one's Queen, frighteningly beautiful, but like a fire, to get too close would end in pain.

'Was it always just only a dream?' Sebastian said, a little angry and raising his voice, 'Was I a convenient amusement to you?' he added, knowing himself this was not true.

Eramia never rose to the bait.

'It would never have worked.'

'I know you love me Eramia, if not, tell me from your own lips.'

Eramia stopped. She turned and met Sebastian as he circled the tree, his dark eyes looked almost fearful of her answer.

'I doubt I will love anyone more,' she began, to Sebastian's surprise, 'but I will only cause us both grief if I for a second longer encourage our affection … It ends here Sebastian. It must, why prolong the inevitable, the impossible agony?'

Sebastian stood there beholding his beloved, but Eramia had turned her head to the side refusing to make eye contact. He had dreaded these words, for Eramia was his first love but actually, his heart was strangely not as pierced through with as many sorrows as he had expected. For part of him felt relief that he could continue to fulfill the vows he had made to God – one of his burdens had been reluctantly lifted. Nevertheless, as he looked at Eramia his heart was also heavy, for he could not imagine even Eve herself to have been more beautiful – he may have stolen a kiss from her but she had stolen his heart forever. Sebastian wept.

Eramia reached out her arm and wiped his tears with her hand. Sebastian closed his eyes; even her touch was so dear to him. Eramia however, managed to fight her emotions, keeping herself from showing her true feelings.

I must be strong, she kept saying to herself, *if I cry now we will never move on or away, with as less pain as possible. He would know how much I loved him.*

Eramia lifted her head to see the sky and drew a deep breath just as Sebastian lifted his pitiable face from the palm of her hand. He saw Eramia's eyes, dry and tearless, and nodded his own head in a forced acceptance. Taking a moment to compose himself, he almost whispered the words,

'My Lady … you will make a fine Queen … if not at great cost to yourself.'

Eramia gave no reply, in either voice or expression, but in her heart she kept repeating, *this is my future, bear it well, start it now.*

Sebastian kissed Eramia's hand, and reluctantly letting go turned and began to walk away. It was there under that elm that Eramia made her first valuable sacrifice; in the silence of the woods, two loved ones parted. Little did Sebastian know how deeply Eramia's heart sorrowed and beat for him alone.

Time was currently a scarce commodity for the dwellers of Greenhaven, their King or Queen included. No sooner had Sebastian left Eramia's presence than Hannah came bounding towards her full of anticipation and talk of activity.

'It will be better than the Great Hall at the feast of St. Andrew,' she exclaimed, 'No palace of grandeur or opulent Hall could compare with the extravagance of nature at dawn!'

Hannah hardly stopped to breathe as she indulged in the details of the next day's glorious ceremony. Eramia smiled graciously and listened to all her friend had to say, but she could not escape from thoughts of Sebastian, then her father and what was unfolding at Tanath.

What will be left? She said to herself, *echoing her father's own concerns. What will become of us when this is all over ... and what will it have made us to become?*

14

The Passing of Orran

Before the sun had risen, the army of Greenhaven kept watch over the mist-covered gloom of the sea. The flag of Sgurr Mhor flew but no one could see it for mist and darkness. The approaching dawn brought coldness with it and Narses rubbed his hands together for warmth. His breath could be seen in the light of the torches, always producing more, always disappearing. All the men fixed their eyes out at sea. Each man waited for a glimpse of the enemy, each one hating the waiting more than the prospect of war.

The sun eventually began to rise but it failed to penetrate the mist as it arched its way into the sky. There was silence at Tanath. Only the breeze could occasionally be heard which was growing in strength and becoming as restless as the men. Narses looked at Valdar who had been thinking for a while that the breeze was ideal for sailing and returned a look of complete agreement.

'There's a storm coming,' said Valdar gravely.

'Aye,' replied Narses, 'and not just in the weather.'

Suddenly, the attention of both men was drawn towards a noise across the cove. They kept looking at each other, then over to the islands at the far end of the bay, and then back to each other.

'There,' said Valdar, 'there it is again.'

Narses violently nodded, listening intently into the wind. Short whistling noises and the vague shouts of men. The warriors of Greenhaven all stood to their feet and everyone ran to the edge of the wall. Narses turned to the man next to him,

'Find the King, war is upon us!' he shouted.

Then out of the mist grew an orange glow, shortly followed by another. At first, some thought it was the sun, until an unknown voice cried out,

'It's the ships; their ships have been set alight! Their ships are on fire!'

A loud cheer broke out from among the men rising high into the morning sky. Valdar, Botherick and Narses knew that once the first or second ship had been attacked, the men on the outer islands would be counter-attacked and flee, leaving the passage free for the other ships to sail through unscathed.

Orran made it to the top of the castle wall just as the first dark outlines of the ships drew nearer. His breathing was heavy and long. As the Men of the North sailed closer, so the rising sun above the clouds cut its way through the morning mist, and by the time they were in striking distance only a faint haze remained on the horizon. The cloud above them was low and grey but out over the sea huge storm clouds gathered. Orran looked down on the bay full of unwanted guests, their ships with sea serpent's heads carved at the front.

Apt, like that serpent of old you shall never totally conquer us, you wicked men who spill the blood of innocents everywhere you go, Orran said to himself.

Orran turned to Valdar and Narses.

'Do not cease fighting them until every last one of them is dead, until their cursed bodies lie on the ocean floor and their broken ships with them.'

He was angry with them, for their arrogance, their violence, their greed, and was almost spitting as he spoke, but not all of his anger was righteous.

'Kill them all,' he cried, 'Let them never know the north again.'

While Narses started positioning his archers in accordance to the number of ships, Orran thought to himself,

If they ever leave this place alive may the Seven Hunters laugh at their destruction! This was a group of unseemly placed islands out to the west, the ocean beat against them relentlessly with high and strong waves.

Orran's present anger tired him more than all the preparation he had done for their attack. The King left the wall for the inner safety of Tanath.

'I will return when the battle becomes most fierce,' he told Narses as he passed him.

'Archers!' Valdar shouted with a voice so loud the whole bay must have heard, 'Prepare to fire.'

Each bowman lit his arrow and placed it on their bow awaiting the next order.

'Archers fire.'

A sound like a mighty wind flew into the air. Valdar, his eyes bulging with anticipation, looked over to Narses who stood looking out to the ships and smiling to himself.

'Aaaahhhh,' Narses shouted into the wind, clenching his fists and tensing his whole body. His eyes were like those of a wild horse and his grin almost demonic.

Some men fight because they have to; others … said Valdar to himself … *their very heart beats for it.*

No sooner had the first round of arrows fell upon their enemies, when a second volley was on the go and an incoming lot approached.

Snap. Crack. Whoosh. Thud.

The thuds were never good, thought Valdar, wincing.

Chaos replaced order, madness replaced sanity, and courage, fear. Ships went up in flames and the men on board clamoured about at dangerous heights with buckets of water extinguishing fires. Small boats left the ships and rowed their way to Tanath. The archers of Castle Tanath either fired or fell. Botherick's men used their catapults to fire rugged chunks of disused masonry into their enemy with considerable effect. Parts of the castle were on fire as the greatly outnumbered men of Tanath tried to hold their defence.

Peace had presently left Greenhaven. In its place were smoke and noise, shouting and massive cracking noises, the constant clutter of arrows, and the deep short thudding sounds of bodies hitting stone floors. The carnage continued for a few hours, Tanath held herself well, the Men of the North found it almost impossible to breach its outer defences, almost, but not quite. So many Men of the North had fallen at the base of the castle's walls trying to climb up ladders into Tanath that they ended up placing the ladders on top of the slain and reducing the height they had to climb: stepping on their own dead to cause the death of others.

The archers were running out of arrows on some parts of the castle wall, and gathering up their enemies' arrows, they returned them with added fire. Over half the ships were ablaze by late afternoon and two had partially sunk. Ninian peeped out of a tiny window that overlooked the bay and could hardly believe how a view which had so often inspired reflection now resembled such a polluted landscape – like an old part of town left to decay.

Ninian sensed the battle grew stronger, there were strange voices somewhere below him and as he turned to flee the room, a ladder filled his view through the small window. He desperately wanted to leave, but knew he could never forgive himself for cowardice. Looking about the room, he noticed a tall iron candlestick at the far side by the door. Ninian ran and grabbed it with both hands. He pushed it through the slit of the window until the candlestick's leg wrapped around one side of the ladder, which at this point shook by the ascending men. With all his might he pushed hard against the ladder causing it to jolt, then bounce, and finally to fall away from the wall. Nevertheless, a foreign tongue wails the same song when faced with death or pain, and Ninian screwed up his face at the thought and consequence of his actions.

I must find Orran, he said to himself, hastily retreating from the room.

'The walled garden's been breached!' bellowed a cry from the corner of the southern wall.

Valdar ran to the edge of the tower from which he was directing his troops and looked down into the garden. Like flies on dead meat, the whole area began to fill up with the enemy. Botherick and his men fought like cornered wolves, with vehement ferocity as if the human had been entirely replaced by the beast. Strike after strike, hacking, chopping, ducking, swinging, metal on metal, iron on iron, and both were sinking into frail flesh. The whole garden smelt of sweat and blood – the trees soaking up the spilt life of men.

The battle, however, was too great.

'Fall back,' cried Valdar, 'Fall back!'

Botherick refused to open the sealed doors from the garden into the castle and risk it being over run, so he fought to the end, an end that was neither quick nor painless.

Where is Dante? Valdar angrily said to himself, as the Men of the North rushed up to the inner garden wall, which was considerably lower than the outer wall. Valdar noted that they were bigger than other men were; by no means giants, but certainly a race built for war.

Narses directed his men to the inner wall of the garden while he went to find Orran.

'My lord,' he said quite breathless from the fight, 'If ever you seek death, now is the time,' his eyebrows raised, his face speckled with blood.

'I fear it is upon me whether I seek it or not,' Orran said, with a glimmer of strength back in his voice.

Narses and Ninian, along with other servants in the room all waited on Orran's next words. Instead of speaking however, he simply stood up and walked towards the door.

'Which part of the castle,' he calmly asked Narses.

'The wall above the garden my lord,' he replied, fixing his eyes on his King's face.

Orran stopped just before the door and turned to see Ninian, who was leaning on his staff with his head down but lifted his eyes to meet those of his old friend. They exchanged a thousand goodbyes and a deeply shared farewell all in silence, with slight nods of their heads and half smiles. Neither believed it was the *very* end, and they shared a comfort void in the life of the godless.

'To war we go,' Orran spoke coolly to Narses, 'lead the way.'

Narses led the King through a number of corridors all filled with memories, each with its own distinct smell. As they ventured down the staircase from the guest's quarters to the door that opened straight onto the wall where the battle raged, the noise of the fighting became almost deafening. Orran stopped before the door. It was solid oak, three layers thick and it took a man of considerable strength to pull it open. Narses put both hands to the task, but before he pulled it open, he said,

'Tell me when, your majesty.'

Orran immediately drew his sword and held it as firm as was possible in front of him. He bore no shield, and he spoke only one more time, as if with the voice of youth returning in abundance.

'As King of all my people, I serve you now. Narses, open the door.'

Narses yanked back the door and a great crack echoed from its seldom-turned hinge, as he moved to the side of the corridor. Narses set his eyes upon the King who passed him in his royal attire, his eyes wide and darting back and forth, his mouth open and teeth clenched.

Orran entered the wall in the thickest part of the battle. He lifted his sword high above his head, and fixing his eyes on his intended victim, forced it down with all the energy he could muster – the sudden end of the motion took all the power out of his arms. He did not even have time to raise his sword again, before, whack – a colossal blow to the head. It was so heavy, and went so deep; it instantly ended all motion, all strength, all thoughts, and all life. Not five seconds had passed from entering the battle and there lay Orran, dead. Slain with countless others, his body helped carpet the wall. No time for final thoughts, no room for last words, no grand final speech, only death, motionless, blood covered death.

Narses pushed the door closed behind him but did not escape seeing his master fall. The servants with him stood there trembling until one of them managed to mutter,

'The King has fallen, Orran is dead! The King is dead!'

Narses put his hand out motioning to him to be quiet.

'It's the nature of the beast my friends,' said Narses, 'War will make a hero of one and meat of another, and if we do not all share his fate he will be mourned for as was fitting for a king, for a good man ... for ...' Narses silently mourned his friend with passed memories.

'What do we do?' asked one of the servants all in a panic, 'What do we do now?'

'Gird yourself with a sword,' replied Narses, 'and let us see if we can be heroes.'

The walls of Tanath were a faithful friend that day, and apart from the breach on the section of the walled garden, she held out the murderous sons of Nebat, those Men of the North. Valdar assembled as many men as possible to the attack where the King had fallen, although

Valdar was unaware of his death. One by one he fought his way through man after man, one on the left, one on the right, then straight ahead, bringing his sword down with power and deadly skill.

The soldiers of Greenhaven regained the wall after forty minutes of arduous battle. They kicked off the ladders from their positions and threw the bodies of their enemies off after them. As the Men of the North fell back to the garden to regroup at the rear of the castle, every soldier who owned a bow turned and faced their fleeing foe. A hail of arrows rained down on them and covered the ground like the falling blossom of the cherry trees in late spring. Unlike the sword, however, few arrows kill a man outright, and as they fell and limped, squirmed on the floor and writhed with pain in contorted heaps on the earth, just at that very point, the small door Botherick was so loath to open flew back its unlocked sides.

Out charged Narses, both hands gripping his sword, and he was followed by the two servants who went with Orran to his death. Then after them, came other servants of the castle, the gardeners, cooks and cleaners, even women, some with axes, others had swords, one had only a spade. They fell upon their wounded prey like lions chasing young foul. In went the swords, the axes, the fists, the boots, and the spade. Off came their heads, out went their life – their greed had consumed them, and for all their want, they had left this earth with nothing, not even dignity.

The household servants cheered and jumped about when the last of their enemy lay at their feet, the cook and the gardener shared a quick dance of victory, but then came a cheer louder than theirs, as the Knights of Greenhaven rejoiced above them on the wall. The servants looked up and saw their captive audience, many of the servants were shaking, full of fear and yet also ecstatic.

'Today, providence has made you heroes,' said Narses smiling to the two servants behind him as they watched the small boats return to the ships half full. Nevertheless, for all their rejoicing, dancing and songs, the ships never left the bay and this caused Valdar an immense deal of unease. Amidst the buoyant celebrations of the garden victory, a solemn cry of lament went up, as the men came across the slain body of Orran, his head almost cleaved from his body. The two cries were both as loud as each other, so that no one could distinguish between the tears of laughter and the tears of sorrow.

Valdar fell upon the King and wept bitterly. Either man or victory would not comfort him. Valdar took the King up in his arms and carried him to Ninian in the Great Hall, where the two tore their clothes and cried out aloud, neither ate nor drank until the sun had set. The castle was bustling with activity as the men repaired the defences; some of the soldiers carved more arrows and collected the ones on the ground and castle doors. The knights grabbed food wherever possible and they cared for the wounded in proportion to their means and ability. They left the dead where they lay for the present, moving only the bodies that caused obstructions on the wall. They prepared for battle again as the ships showed no sign of leaving. When night approached, it came with a thick darkness that hung over Tanath and those who were awake could virtually feel it. Smoke drifted in the low clouds like the thoughts of the mind in the heart of man. Some of the knights sat around with a fixed stare, others were laughing, and a few prayed; those that could, slept.

15

The Coronation of
Queen Eramia

A solitary lark made known the approaching dawn; it woke Eramia who embraced the cool morning with a few deep breaths. It was still fairly dark when the eager lark encouraged his friends to join him in song, yet Hannah had been up for a while and Eramia thought Hannah was the more excited of the two. For years, they had talked of this day, but now it had arrived, different from all their expectations. Eramia thought Hannah was right – what setting for a coronation could be grander than nature itself? There was something simple and innocent about it, yet there was also something excitingly savage about it too. It spoke to Eramia of her ancestors, which caused within her an immense sense or responsibility.

Eramia was not just the Queen of Greenhaven, the sovereign of her people; she was a keeper of heritage, a custodian of traditions and a steward of history. She was not only safeguarding Greenhaven's future, but also the kingdom's past. Despite all the responsibility that she would bear, coupled with the knowledge of her own weakness, Eramia was sure of her calling.

Eramia soon realized that Hannah was not the only person who was awake and up before her, in fact, between the trees she noticed quite a lot of movement. Dark shapes moving this way and that, carrying things and returning for more, and this intrigued her immensely and she went over to investigate. As Eramia stood up to move, Dante appeared from nowhere and joined her.

'They're nearly finished,' he said, 'early for a feast I know, but fitting for the occasion.'

As they moved nearer to the open space of Glamondon, Eramia could make out some of what was happening. The parting of the cover of the trees added light to the scene. Right down the centre of Glamondon there now stood an impressively long stone table – huge slabs of stone spread with vibrant lichens and moss lay balanced across equally placed rocks. Tree stumps of various types and sizes lined either side of the table, and at the head of the table, stood a large stone throne. The throne had an impressive stag's head attached to the top and deer skins covering the seat and arms. It was crude, but Eramia loved it. A hive of activity surrounded the table and on to it, the people placed all manner of foods on wooden plates and in stone bowls: apples, pears, mushrooms, berries, nuts, meat, bread, cheese and honey, water, wine and milk in abundance.

The Silent Shadow has certainly learnt how to live off the land, thought Eramia with joyful wonder.

Hannah came up behind Eramia and placed on her head a crown of intertwined flowers, delicate to the eye and subtle of scent, small blue flowers with a few intermingled white ones, then she handed her mistress a few hand picked bluebells.

Eramia took the flowers off her head to view her friend's handiwork.

'It's beautiful,' she said.

'And more comfortable than any gold crown,' Hannah replied, smiling brightly.

Hannah then took Eramia by the hand, leading her off into the bushes.

'Come on,' she urged, 'you must start getting ready. What are the cleanest clothes you have?' inquired Hannah.

Eramia thought for a while,

'My blue dress is least visibly dirty,' she laughed.

'Blue it is.'

Eramia sought out some undergrowth in which to change, and the change was noticeable. As hardy as Eramia was, she was still mindful of her upbringing in the King's court and she knew how to dress well in fine clothes. She looked utterly resplendent emerging from the early morning sunlit forest, with her long sapphire dress and crown of nature's glory. The beams of sunlight fell through the gaps in the trees picking up marvelously the rich dew soaked forest palette. Eramia wore her hair in two long plaits which fell down the front of her shoulders, and Hannah fixed some of the white flowers she had used for Eramia crown in her mistress's dark hair as if she carried the stars themselves.

Although a lot of activity encircled Glamondon that dawn, it was not long before Comasius called for Eramia to come forward to become Queen. The Silent Shadow members all gathered on the ancient rock in a half moon crescent and looked to the place in the trees from where Eramia approached.

A few moments passed before the branches of the trees and bushes started moving, and then they caught glances of her amid the green foliage, until Eramia stood totally exposed before them all. She walked out slowly onto Glamondon, Hannah a few paces behind, her head bowed. Everyone bowed their heads, but only Sebastian kept his eyes firmly fixed on his loved one, his Queen. Eramia was the most beautiful female ever seen in the woods by the Silent Shadow, she seemed to them as if the glories of nature had achieved its pinnacle with her presence. Sebastian was by no means the only man present that morning who loved her, however tainted by lust.

As Eramia approached, the Silent Shadow and Sebastian walked out to meet her. Sebastian was the only ordained man among them that morning, and it was his responsibility to confirm Eramia in her new office as Queen. There were promises to make before God and man, for it was certainly no light matter to become sovereign of Greenhaven. Sebastian read the traditional ordination ceremony text from the book that Ninian had passed to Dante. With the sun still shinning upon them among the gathering clouds, and the birds bearing witness with their songs on this ancient traditional service, Sebastian read the last lines in unison with all the people.

'The tears that you shed in righteousness for your people here, may surely find you again as the dew which will refresh you in heaven. Amen.'

Sebastian slowly closed the small leather book in his hand and nodded to Dante who stood just to the left of Eramia along with Comasius. Dante raised both his hands in the air and with a loud voice proclaimed,

'Behold your Queen! Eramia, Queen of Greenhaven, honour her!'

While Dante said these words, the whole gathering knelt before her.

'Arise,' Eramia said. 'Even in this hour of imminent danger, we share in a ceremony which is also a celebration. Let us feast on this most happy morning as if it were our last, for I fear for some of us, it may will be! Enjoy this meal that is set before you.'

'Amen,' croaked Comasius, 'Would you bless this table?' he asked Sebastian, who gave thanks to God.

Everyone sat down and ate and drank until their hearts were merry or content or both. The forest had rarely known such joviality among the sons of men, the overlapping sounds of chewing and drinking, talking, laughing, the cracking of nuts and the occasional murmur of a song that suddenly spilt over into tumultuous singing. The sparrows that had eagerly coveted the contents of the table hung back, while the squirrels, so desperate for some nuts, dared not venture down from their trees, as the riotous banquet was consumed. The only darkness that morning was found in the crows that flew in to join them and scavenge what they could from the floor around the table.

Even Sebastian enjoyed his time around the stone table, in many ways it felt like one of the celebratory feasts he had shared back at the monastery of Ness. This pleased Eramia very much; she knew that in her heart she had caused him deep pain because her own heart shared it equally. Every now and again Eramia darted a glance at Sebastian but was very careful nobody was watching. She helped herself to a plate of juicy berries and thought back to the first time she had laid eyes on him, and sighed within herself.

Of all the men to capture my heart, she contemplated.

'Isn't it all just wonderful!' chirped Hannah, who sat to the left of Eramia. 'Who would believe all of this?' she exclaimed, opening her arms over the table, the food and its guests. 'There were moments on the journey that caused me to be more fed up or tired than I have ever been before,' Hannah continued, 'but then a moment such as this comes along … and I've never felt more alive.'

Eramia smiled at her friend, and then looked at Sebastian who had also been listening to Hannah.

'Isn't it often the way? Eramia remarked, 'that the most precious of blessings shine through from the darkest of circumstances, if we would but just wait for them to be revealed.'

Dante, who was sitting to the right of Eramia next to Comasius, had also been listening to what Eramia said.

'Then perhaps there are greater blessings yet to come, for to be sure, a thick darkness awaits us all when this supper has ended.'

The faces of those who heard Dante became quite solemn quite quickly. For a short time, they had forgotten what that last supper was in aid of and why they were eating it. None of them could in all honesty be angry with Dante, for he did not lie in what he said, but the spirit of those who heard him became downcast.

'Your thoughts are never too far from wars are they Dante?' Hannah asked him, a little disgruntled.

Dante looked at her with contempt.

'These are no matters for your concern. What part to play do you have on the battlefield?'

'My bow is as good as any man's,' Hannah foolishly replied, raising her voice just enough for the rest of the table to stop their conversations and listen.

'It's not your bow that concerns me,' said Dante.

'Meaning?'

'You are no more than a girl … your bow will be led by how your heart feels, not by your hand, not by what needs to be done.'

'And your hands feel differently to mine, I suppose?'

'Enough!' Dante growled, standing up and banging the table with both fists. 'Yes, … yes, my hands will feel the sword that will break through and sink into other men's flesh, hands that will feel the sweat and blood and lifeless bodies of those they have slain. Is that what you want your hands to feel? Is it? Because believe me woman, once they have felt it there will be stains on those hands that will never be washed away.'

A moments silence encircled the table, bar the cawing of the crows that all flew back a few feet when Dante rose to his feet.

Comasius broke the silence.

'Dante is in part correct, young lady. It is not your task to fight, but to serve your mistress and that has an honour of its own …'

He would have carried on but Eramia unexpected interrupted him.

'And what if her mistress chooses to fight?

Not only was everyone silent, but the cups and knives and food were all put down by those who held them, the people's eyes darting back and forth from Eramia to Comasius.

'My Lady …' Comasius began, his voice quite weak.

'Is not your King to lead you out in battle? Why not your Queen?' Eramia continued, over the top of Comasius.

The gathering all looked around the table at each other. Hannah childishly smirked at Dante.

'Were you going to leave us in the woods?' Eramia carried on.

'Of course you were coming with us, but you were not, and will not, fight,' replied Dante. 'And if you intend to, I will not – I will not be responsible for leading you to your death.'

'Do I not have a voice? Am I not your Queen? Or is the Silent Shadow considering another change of monarchy?'

'Don't be insolent Eramia,' Comasius said, for the first time looking close to angry. 'Yes, you are our Queen, and we would like to keep you as such! It is dangerous enough for you merely traveling with us, let alone to confront the Men of the North. No, no, no, it just won't be tolerated.'

Dante could not resist a quick glance back at Hannah who he knew would be infuriated. Hannah screwed up her face and shook her head at Dante, then turned towards Eramia.

Eramia rose from her seat, this caused the seriously annoyed Dante to sit back down. Comasius placed his aged scrawny hand on Dante's shoulder and squeezed it a couple of times. Comasius was fully behind Dante on this occasion.

Eramia looked the length of the table – all eyes were fixed on her, Sebastian's, for the wrong reason.

'It appears the celebratory spirit has come to an end,' she began sarcastically, which raised a few smiles.

Before she spoke another word, the most curious of incidents occurred. A man came running out of the woods, severely breathless and sweating. He was wearing only trousers and shoes, both made of skins, and his body bore strange marks. Neither knew who was most shocked, Eramia and the Silent Shadow by the unexpected arrival of the uninvited guest, or the man who had stumbled out of the trees into a feast, held before normal breakfast time on a huge stone table with the presence of a Queen.

When the man's eyes fell upon Dante he let out a sigh of relief, for the stranger was of the Ghindred and had crossed paths with Dante in the past.

'They're on the move sir,' he shouted, 'all of them, hundreds, they're all moving, and they started off yesterday!'

Everyone firmly fixed their eyes on Dante.

'How many exactly?' asked Dante.

'Hard to say,' he said, trying to catch his breath, 'four hundred or there about.'

'Four hundred!' exclaimed Sebastian, 'that's ten times our number!'

'Sir, that's not quite true,' the savage looking man said, 'for I am one of the runners sent to gather the Ghindred to fight and there are about fifty or so who we think would be willing.'

'And remember my regiment is at least still forty strong,' added Dante.

Sebastian still was not overly reassured with the new odds.

'Friend, remind me of your name,' Dante inquired.

'Benaiah.'

'Go Benaiah, gather the Ghindred together and bring them by way of the old funeral path. Find my regiment and take them with you, but leave the horses. Here, take my ring so that they know I have sent you, and move fast Benaiah. Meet us on the beach at Tanath, staying unseen until we get there. Do you understand? You must stay out of sight.'

Benaiah nodded.

'Good, than go at once, God give you speed.'

Benaiah turned to leave, but Eramia stood behind him so that he came close to colliding with her.

'Here, take some water first,' she said, offering him a cup which he gladly received.

Benaiah opened his mouth wide and drank it in seconds.

'Bless you my Lady,' he said, handing Eramia back the cup and grabbing some food, before running off once more into the woods.

Eramia watched him disappear into the trees.

'Eramia, we must leave at once,' said Dante.

'I know, I know,' Eramia said disturbed.

'We leave in ten minutes,' Dante shouted, turning round to the rest of the table.

'Will Benaiah be safe?' Eramia asked, grabbing Dante's forearm.

'He is one of the mountain men and they are hardy types, he will be fine,' said Dante, with a tone of respect, 'now let's get going.'

Every man darted from the table to gather his things, except Comasius who was far too old and frail for the likes of war, or even long journeys. Sadness covered his face and Eramia asked him what was wrong, while Hannah packed up Eramia's things.

'All my life I have lived for adventure, a life full of danger and risk, now comes the main act of this story and I'm too old and haggard to take part,' he said, all fed up.

'But without your parts, your scenes in the play, this part of the story would never have existed at all. And some men are called to be faithful, not great, not heroic on the battlefield, still, I think the former calling to be the harder of the two, for its fruits are not easily as seen … not yet, anyway,' Eramia replied.

'Go, your Majesty,' he said with the slightest of smiles, 'I think on your part both may yet be seen.'

16

Death on the Beach

The journey back through the woods, forest glades and valleys of Greenhaven, proved hard going for Dante, Eramia and the Silent Shadow. All the pleasantness they could have enjoyed from the natural ruggedness of the surrounding area was taken away by the speed in which they wished to accomplish their task. They pushed on hard, moving right through the night, which was made easier by the frequent illumination of the moon's light through the broken clouds. However, they were aware all too often of what they were hastening towards.

The party ate on the way and drank from every river and stream they came across, but even the Silent Shadow were feeling the strain of the sleepless journey and many worried they would have little strength left to fight. Dante, however, had not been in charge of the armies of Greenhaven for nothing. He knew that if the Men of the North had come across their horses first, the battle was as good as over, so when he had led the others to where his regiment had left the horses, he set a guard and let the men rest. They entered an old run down barn to sleep and gathered as much straw as they could for comfort. Some of the men took off their capes or furs for Eramia and Hannah. Both women and Sebastian fell asleep straight away, even amidst all their anxious thoughts.

Sebastian was severely troubled in his heart. The silence on the recently finished passage through the woods accentuated the voices in his head.

Will I fight or wont I? he kept asking himself in his dreams.

He kept regretting his vow never to kill with the sword again, but would then remember Rastko's face, and believe he had done the right thing. He also knew he would not stand by and let anyone harm Eramia. In so thinking, Sebastian continuously remained in a state of disturbing dilemmas. He knew, as much as the others, that the time for thinking would soon be replaced with a time for action, when the true Sebastian would be revealed to all, including himself.

Hannah awoke at one point as Sebastian nudged her while tossing and turning on the crispy hay. Hannah's heart moved within her as she gazed upon her mistress knowing she was heading towards a battle. In the course of their journey and peril, the Lady she served had only ever been refined by the events that met them on their way. Hannah never envied the beauty of her mistress and she watched her sleep on the hay, her blue dress draped in furs, one arm above her head and the other across her thin waist. Hannah felt nothing but honoured by her calling in life, for in all her serving she felt liberated. She gently stroked Eramia's hair from off her face and lying back down fell asleep once more, warm and unafraid.

One of the Silent Shadow abruptly woke Eramia and her subjects.

'Move, move, move,' Dante repeatedly said, striding around the barn lightly kicking the others from their slumber.

'They are nearly on top of us,' he urged them, 'no more than half a mile away.'

Everyone scrambled to their horses and headed towards Tanath. Sebastian helped Eramia mount her horse and Torridon did the same for Hannah. As they left the barn on the periphery of the small hamlet of Ferntower, a few of the remaining inhabitants waited to see them off on the edge of the road. Some of the local people had water, others small cakes of raisins, and loaves, and some only had bunches of wild flowers to give, but they bowed their heads to these courageous men. Their future depended on their valour.

Dante called over a young boy.

'Have you seen anyone pass by this way lately lad?'

'Some poor looking people come from the woods and spoke to the soldiers, but I wasn't allowed to go near them, then they all left.'

'When was this?'

'Only yesterday sir.'

'Good lad, here,' he said, offering him part of his cake, which the small boy took, running back to his mother.

The folk from Ferntower ran off into the glens.

Dante kicked his horse hard, 'To Tanath,' he shouted, and set off in a gallop towards the castle. The rest followed suit, those who had never ridden a horse before doubled up with others, but there were not many that shared. Eramia and Hannah had been riding from their youth and easily kept pace with Dante, and it was always better to be nearer the front of the crowd, as the dust cloud was reduced significantly compared to the rear of the horde. Although riding for a long time was in itself tiring, the very fact they were riding on horses rather than on foot, cheered everyone up.

The sky, however, became ominously dark. There was no rain, but the wind blew increasingly strong the nearer the coast they reached. What with the noise of the movement of the horses as well as the wind, it became increasingly hard to hear anyone speak, and so for the most part, the journey's entertainment became solely the imaginations of the mind.

Before they had arrived at the crest of the hill that would lead them down to the carnage that surrounded Tanath, Dante ordered the Silent Shadow to dismount and walk the last mile and a half by way of the trees at the side of the road. By doing this, he was hoping that the Men of the North aboard the ships would not see them, and that he may come across his regiment and the other Ghindred at the same time. When they started the descent to the beach, a small clearing appeared among the trees enabling them to look over the whole bay. The men's eyes widened when they saw all the ships around Tanath and the wisps of smoke still rising from certain quarters of the castle.

Some members of the Silent Shadow had not left the Eastern Woods for over twenty years and the shear crowdedness of the scene below caused them to become uneasy. Nevertheless, they continued heading down towards where they would take their stand. As they reached the large rocks where the trees became sparse, Dante met his regiment and the Ghindred who had assembled to fight. Most of the fighting men were sleeping, reserving their energy for the exhausting business of war. Dante suggested to Eramia and the others that they joined them as soon as they could.

'It will be a day's journey before our enemy comes if they remain on foot,' he added, 'Get your strength back up while you can.'

Dante went to speak with his regiment commander and Benaiah.

'Does anyone know we are here? Has anyone seen you?'

'Not that we are aware of,' Benaiah replied.

'Good,' said Dante, 'Keep it that way. Benaiah, you have done well, pick a friend you trust who can swim well, at nightfall he will swim across to Tanath and tell … tell … Valdar what to expect from those Men of the North who are coming by foot. And tell him not to leave the sea facing walls void of defence, as we shall fight this battle on Tanath's behalf.'

Then Dante went and found a place where he could sleep, sheltered from the wind and relatively under cover. The night remained cloudy, bringing a dense darkness with it, the wind, if anything increased in power, as if even the elements were becoming violent, getting in the mood for the coming events. Hannah and Sebastian lay fast asleep at the foot of a bulky wind beaten rock, but the noise of the wind in the trees and just being back at Tanath in such foreign circumstances prevented Eramia from joining her friends in sleep.

Later in the night, Eramia sat up, leaning with her aching back against the rock she had been sleeping against, opposite from where Sebastian still slept. Eramia wished she did not have to be so strong all of the time. She longed to be weak enough to take Sebastian for herself, knowing it would be wrong. Her conscience, however, was and always had been tender. She crawled over closer to Sebastian's body and gently stroked his hair away from his eyes – he seemed so at peace.

Eramia continued looking at him, with his youthful vigour and un-spoilt naturalness. She shed a tear and placed her hand over her mouth so as not to wake him.

Wiping her tears from her eyes, she bent down and kissed his forehead.

'I love you so much,' she said, in barely a whisper, before rising up and moving away and letting him sleep.

As Eramia moved around the corner of the rock from where she currently hid in the shadow, she walked straight into Dante who also could not sleep with the noise of the wind. Eramia hung her head low, covering her face with both hair and the darkness of the night.

'The night is far spent, the day is at hand,' Dante said, 'I wonder for how many this night, this sleep, was their last?'

For the next short while neither of them spoke a word to each other, they both just gazed out to Tanath, which they could barely see across the beach and short stretch of water. The wind howled and Eramia shivered aloud.

'Do we have a plan?' she inquired of Dante.

'Oh yes,' Dante began, 'We've called it trying to stay alive!' He laughed to himself as if it was his last form of defence.

Eramia looked at him sternly, she was in no mood for his humour, and Dante clearly saw this as Eramia flicked back her hair and stared straight at him.

'Forgive me, Your Majesty,' he said, trying not to laugh, 'we will wait until the Men of the North have marched almost to the beach, let their sailing friends think their plan will work at last. Then, when I give the signal, we shall run out from both ends of the beach and take our stand between them and Tanath. Half our number shall wait on the beach, the other half will attack on horseback from behind.'

'And my role in all of this?' inquired Eramia.

'You shall oversee the battle from the rear of those who take their stand on the beach, so that you are between us and Tanath. A small rowing boat will wait for you and if the battle gets too close you get in that boat without delay and head straight for the Castle, their boats are too big to get among these rocks when the tide is not fully in, then you'll be safe … well, safer,' he added, wanting to be realistic.

Without warning, Eramia changed the subject and was very blunt in her speech.

'Do you remember that morning back in the woods when I woke up first and you were standing unseen by the tree?

Dante did and he motioned to her with a slight movement of his head to continue.

'I thought back then that you may have had feelings for me.'

Dante's eyebrows rose considerably.

'Oh I know now you do not,' Eramia quickly added, 'I know you did not want to tell me that my father was dying and … well … was that why you were so angry when we first left?'

'Aye, it was, but when we first left I did not think you were ready for what I knew was ahead. I had always viewed you as being so delicate, the girl I have watched grow and flourish … now you are a woman and you have a strength some men would envy. Not only that, but you are a Queen and seeing you at your coronation I knew you were ready and if anything, it was I who was not ready for you!'

'Are you ready for what is coming this day?' Eramia asked.

Dante stared at the Queen with his dark steely gaze.

'The smaller the odds, the greater the glory,' he said deeply.

When the two of them had finished speaking about Dante's plans and the coming day, they realized others were also up and engaged in conversation, and at some unknown point, the day had broken in on them. Dante took Eramia's hand and kissed it.

'I'll put everyone in position … be of good courage, your majesty, your father would be so very proud of you.'

The next hour or so involved people moving into positions, and putting on armour, grabbing food when and where they could, and sharpening weapons. As it was, their preparation time was scarce and most of the troops were still tired from their journey to the beach. The time for preparing, however, came to a sudden end when the marching beat of four hundred men broke over the top of the hill and descended on Castle Tanath.

Those men of Dante's regiment who waited on horses moved back into the woods so no one would see them. The Men of the North raised a cheer when they saw their fellow men marching and looking unstoppable, storming towards a seemingly easy victory. The enemies of Greenhaven who were on board the ships, those who had failed to take the castle alone yesterday, once more began attacking the castle with a bombardment of arrows. From that point on, everything started to gather pace.

A deep blow of a ram's horn saw the Silent Shadow clamber out from among the rocks at one side of the beach, and the Ghindred run out from the trees on the other side. The Silent Shadow and Ghindred met as one force right in front of Tanath and right in front of the path of the approaching Men of the North. This time there were loud shouts coming from the partially ruined walls of Tanath. Some of the soldiers defending the walls immediately ran and got some new flags and raised them up over Tanath's towers, others blew trumpets as if they had won a victory. Nevertheless, those small actions instilled fresh bravery in those who stood on the beach between Tanath and possible, even likely, death.

The Men of the North marched straight towards them. They carried double-edged axes and large round shields of leather on wood with brass rivets. Their helmets were decorated in the shape of sea serpent's heads and their clothes were of vibrant reds. The Silent Shadow and the Ghindred carried little or no protection in terms of armour; they only carried weapons such as swords, spears and bows. To these giant warriors of the north they must have appeared like children, but even a child, when cornered, can prove quite ferocious.

Dante was on the beach close to Eramia, Hannah and Sebastian. Sebastian was reluctant to draw his sword until his enemy reached a distance of no less than fifty feet from his position; then his basic drive for the survival of Eramia took over. He drew his sword from its sheath and held it out in front of him. Hannah stood directly in front of Eramia, her bow drawn and arrow in place. Dante gave a shout of command for those who had arrows to fire, and the archers only just heard him over the powerful winds.

As the first torrent of arrows flew into the marching Men of the North, Dante blew once more on the ram's horn, long and hard. Eramia watched the road some way above the enemy as the horsemen from Dante's regiment rode into formation and sped down to their aid. With all the noise of marching feet, firing of arrows and gushing of wind, the Men of the North did not notice that they were under attack from behind until Greenhaven's cavalry was almost on top of them. It was too late by this time for them to form any organized defence. Those at the back of the invaders had time only to turn round and cry aloud, some for help, some from fear.

Dante's regiment rode straight into the confused rear ranks of their enemy, each bore a spear with a small white flag attached to its head and the shield of Greenhaven emblazoned on it. As soon as the horsemen cut through the Men of the North from behind, the Silent Shadow and the other Ghindred ran upon them from the front. Those horsemen, who had not been knocked off their horses or wounded, carried on riding, some were bearing left and others were bearing right. Turning at opposite ends of the beach, they rode in formation like geese migrating, one section attacking the front half of the line of foreign soldiers and one section headed for what was left of the rear. All uniformity of ranks among the Men of the North disappeared as the horsemen wreaked havoc from every direction. With each wave of attack however, fewer and fewer mounted horses remained, until they fought the battle entirely on foot, spread out right across the beach.

As the battle drew closer to Eramia, Dante moved forward adding effortlessly to the number of men he had slain. He kept shouting back,

'To Tanath Eramia, to Tanath, go!'

But as Eramia and Hannah turned to wade out to the rowing boat, four huge beast-like men flanked Dante and came directly towards them.

'Go,' shouted Sebastian, 'Hurry,' pushing them towards the boat, 'Go now.'

While the boat edged away from the beach, the four men reached the edge of the shore and Sebastian turned round to face them. He kept looking at them as they approached, then he turned back to see how far Eramia had gone in the boat, and then back to the Men of the North. Eramia and Hannah finally struggled into the little wooden boat as the wind drove it further from the beach, and they set about rowing to Tanath with the little deaf man who had brought Sebastian across the water to the castle the last time he visited. Eramia and Hannah were still dangerously close to the battle and in easy reach of a stray arrow.

Sebastian turned to face his enemy, no longer checking behind him at his loved one's progress. He swung his sword from side to side, knee deep in the rough waves breaking the length of the beach. There was no question in his mind now about whether or not he should fight. He brought his sword down hard, striking the lower back of one man and the shoulder blade of another, whilst being knocked down into the seaweed filled ocean swell. Despite the fact that he was struggling to his feet once more, he remembered Rastko, and he made sure both wounded men would never get up again. Back in went his sword.

The two other men bypassed Sebastian heading for the boat with the women in it, but gave up chasing the vessel when the water rose above their waists. They turned and made their way back towards Sebastian, approaching him from behind, one on his left, the other on his right, and Eramia drifting further towards the castle and safety. Sebastian could clearly see Eramia in the boat behind the two men. Now that she was safe, and he was sure nothing would come of their love, his vow rushed back violently to the forefront of his thinking, and Sebastian lowered his sword, weeping. The two foreign warriors stood there, both hands gripping their axes, infuriated by the deaths of their friends by Sebastian's hand. The two men moved towards him. Sebastian fell to his knees with his sword resting in the silt, propping him up among the wind and the roaring waves. The lifeless bludgeoned bodies of the two men he had just killed brushed against him as the waves relentlessly crashed upon the shore. There was no strength left in him to raise his sword again, but his will and his conscience were flooded with peace.

Eramia and Hannah watched in horror from the little boat as Sebastian's two foes mercilessly strode towards him – yet he did not speak a word, nor move a muscle. As the two axes of his enemies rose above his defenceless body, Sebastian simply closed his eyes and lifted his head towards heaven.

'Forgive me Lord,' he prayed.

No!' cried Eramia, long and thunderous, 'No, Sebastian! Sebastian!'

Hannah had to physically stop Eramia falling in the ocean swell as she was reaching so far out of the boat to Sebastian and screaming. Her screaming fell on deaf ears, as the life of the saint that she loved so much, no longer dwelt in the body that now floated in the cold foaming waters of the seashore, the seaweed made black by the reddening of the water. Sebastian had both saved her and left her and Eramia could do nothing but howl uncontrollably, weeping bitterly until her eyes were sore and her body weak. Hannah held Eramia tightly in her arms as the little deaf man rowed his hardest to arrive at the castle.

The battle on the beach raged on, but when the Men of the North realized that their brethren in the ships still failed to take the castle, they lost heart and ran down the peninsula to try to board one of the ships as they sailed back out to sea. The most damaged of the ships that could still sail had already started to withdraw. As the tide went out some of the soldiers from the castle came out to help finish the struggle on the beach. There were only eleven men left alive from the Silent Shadow, the Ghindred and Dante's regiment added together. Torridon had fallen, as had Benaiah. Dante, for all his recklessness, remained totally unscathed.

The sea played a vicious host to the Men of the North that day, brutally driving some of the vessels into the rocks at the end of the bay. The battle was over; Greenhaven had won, but so, so very much had been lost. The deaf man managed to bring Eramia and Hannah to the castle safely after some considerable effort.

'Where is my father?' asked Eramia, standing in the large courtyard of the castle, 'Where is Sebastian? Where is …?' her voice failed as she railed against all that had happened. The battle had left an indelible mark on the young monarch; she had now witnessed the most grotesque aspects of being Queen.

Ninian heard of Eramia's return and rushed out of the tower to meet her. He threw his arms around Eramia who stood their motionless, she was too exhausted and in shock to hug Ninian in return. He placed his arm around her shoulder and led her away from the courtyard and into the castle. Ninian tried to comfort Eramia but he knew from his own experience that now was not the time for words.

Instead, Ninian took Eramia to the Great Hall where her father had been placed on the central slab of rock. Orran's broken body lay on top of a sea-green cloth draped over the large slab. Eramia knelt down beside her father. She touched his frail looking face that was as cold as her hands. Eramia stared helplessly at the royal armour that encased the man who raised her and the burden that she now felt as Queen almost crushed her already fragile spirit.

'He was a faithful King,' said Ninian, his eyes filling with water.

'He was a faithful father,' Eramia replied, wiping away the tears that fell on Orran's pale rough skin.

'And what about Sebastian, any news?' Ninian asked reluctantly.

Eramia lowered her head until it rested on the breastplate of her father's armour and could not speak for crying. Eramia's anguish caused Ninian to fall back onto one of the chairs and the old man broke down in tears.

'Such a waste,' cried Ninian, 'he was so young … so young … he would have been so useful to you now that you are Queen … he was so faithful.'

Eramia slowly nodded.

'I know,' she said, weeping bitterly, 'he was dying to be faithful.'

Printed in the United Kingdom by
Lightning Source UK Ltd., Milton Keynes
R978900001B/R9789PG138716UKX27B/19/P